Madelyn of the Sky

Book 1: Stones and Swords
Book 2: Skyships and Sisters
Book 3: Fire and Frostburn
Book 4: Rescue and Rage
Book 5: Queens and Chaos
Book 6: Alliances and Endings

MADELYN of the SKY

SKYSHIPS AND SISTERS

JONATHON MAST

Dawnsbrook

DAWNSBROOK PRESS

Cover art and cover design by Ian Samson

Published by Dawnsbrook Press

dawnsbrook.com

CARANGTH'S SHIP

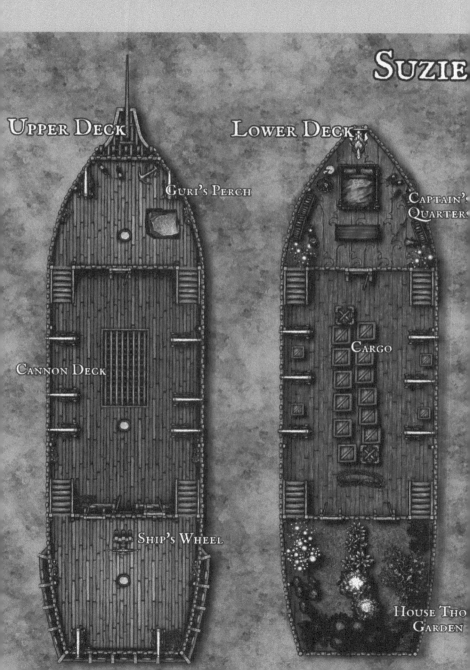

SUZIE

UPPER DECK

GURI'S PERCH

CANNON DECK

SHIP'S WHEEL

LOWER DECK

CAPTAIN'S
QUARTERS

CARGO

HOUSE THO
GARDEN

PROLOGUE

Thunder cracked the sky. White fingers of lightning strained toward the ship. The sky-ship rocked in the terrible wind. Cold bit into every inch of the crew's exposed skin.

The captain narrowed his eyes. "A little more speed, boys!" he called.

His crew responded. They scrambled to the sails. Some climbed to the canopy that held them aloft.

"We can't let them catch us!" the captain roared. The wind whipped at his long red coat. He frowned. "Bring me the chest."

A few of the crew ran belowdecks. Soon, they hauled a heavy wooden chest onto the deck and let it fall before the captain.

"Gjemb," he summoned.

A woman stood at his shoulder. "Aye."

"Open it."

She nodded and turned toward the chest. The top blossomed, as if the entire thing had been a bud on a plant. Petals opened to reveal an empty space.

The captain nodded. "Aye." He stepped forward. "We paid for these dearly. We won't let them have them back, will we?"

"No, Captain," the woman answered.

"Good." He reached inside his coat and took out a long package wrapped in heavy canvas. "They'll be safe here." He bent to place the package into the chest. As he did, the fabric shifted. Something metal fell out. It grazed the captain's wrist.

He hissed. The package clattered to the deck. He glared at it. Smoke rose from the captain's blackened skin.

"Captain!" one of the crew called. "The storm's catching up!"

"Course it is," he answered. "Why wouldn't it?" He stooped and scooped up the package, making sure none of its contents touched his exposed skin. He dumped it into the chest. "Gjemb, close it up."

The woman nodded. The chest closed, every petal going back where it had been before.

2

"Now," the captain said as he turned to gaze at the pursuing storm, "we need to find safe harbor. Someplace House Tempest won't find us."

Something green flashed in the distance.

He narrowed his eyes. "Safe harbor." He leaped to the wheel. "Coming about!" he roared. "We'll follow that light. If it's not safe harbor, I'll wager it'll at least get us away from this lot!"

The crew cheered.

The skyship turned toward where the flash of green had been. Soon, it passed over a Bridge and sailed on to someplace very different.

Someplace that hadn't seen a fae skyship in a very, very long time.

Someplace human.

CHAPTER ONE

H ey! Pay attention!" Miah barked.

Madelyn jumped. "Sorry."

"When you're working metal, you need your eyes on it, not over there." Miah sighed. "You're the one who wanted to learn blacksmithing."

"Yeah. Sorry. Yeah." She refocused on the forge. She pumped the bellows that blew air into it, doing her best to keep the temperature even.

Miah shook his head. "What is it this time?"

"I saw a pigeon."

"Plenty of those on the Island. They make a good lunch." He drew out a glowing ingot, squinted at it, placed it back into the forge.

"It was flying from Essica's."

"She let one get away, did she? Well, lunch for someone else, then." He went about his business, perfectly at ease.

"How come you never sweat? It's always so hot in here."

Miah chuckled. "You get used to the heat, learn to ignore it. It's how you learn how to pay attention, too. Once you've been burned often enough, you know what you need to watch." He paused. "Like making sure you keep pumping the bellows evenly."

Madelyn kept working the bellows, shaking sweat from her face.

"So what's wrong with a pigeon flying from Essica's?" Miah asked.

"It was a messenger pigeon. She's sending Grandma a message."

"Ah." Miah pulled the ingot out again and nodded. "Keep pumping." He moved to an anvil and hammered the metal twice, three times, and nodded again. Back into the forge the metal went. "What's wrong with our wisewoman sending your grandma a message?"

"She's probably going to tell Grandma that I'm not working hard enough."

"Well, why shouldn't your grandma know the truth?" he replied evenly. "Just because she's helping Prince Aralane run Kenevir down there doesn't mean she doesn't care about you up here on the

Island you set in the sky for us." He waited for the metal to heat again. "Steady with the bellows!"

"Hey!" Madelyn sputtered. "I'm working plenty hard! I've got wisewoman lessons with Essica. Blacksmithing with you. Peter's teaching me about fae stuff since Grandma isn't here to do it. I'm constantly taking people up and down so they can get more supplies. I'm scouting for more refugees. Don't you think that's enough?"

"Not if you're going to lead this Island. We need someone who knows what it is to work hard. Not just some adventurer." He removed the ingot and turned to the anvil again. A few more hammer beats, and then back into the forge.

"I'm not just some adventurer."

"Really?" Miah shook his shaggy head. "If your grandma didn't force all these lessons, what would you be doing?"

Madelyn didn't answer. She didn't want to. She felt the silence stretch as Miah waited. "I'd be saving more people," she finally admitted.

"Exactly." Back to the anvil. More hammering. Back into the forge. He worked in a steady, unhurried rhythm. "But saving them doesn't do anyone any good if the Island's falling apart. We don't just need a hero. We need a leader. Someone who knows the people. Someone who will guide and make sure that everyone has what they need." He sighed and took the ingot out again. "A good leader needs to know how to smith. Not metal. But people. Some people need to be dealt with and hammered into shape. Others need time to cool after coming out of the fire. Or they just need to be heard and given some way to be useful. You need to evaluate people like I do metal. To know where to pound, where to work, and where to simply leave something be. How to guide and shape people so they can all work together."

"Well, maybe I'm not that person," Madelyn whispered. Maybe she wasn't someone who could lead. Maybe she just wanted to go and rescue people.

Miah didn't respond.

Someone rushed into the blacksmithing hut. She gasped for air. "Madelyn!"

Madelyn dropped the bellows and rushed to the newcomer's side.

"Hey!" barked Miah, but Madelyn ignored him.

"Renity!" she said. "What's wrong?"

"I was out checking the crops. And I saw something in the sky."

7

"Dragons?" Madelyn's stomach dropped. They'd been lucky with dragons before, but that's exactly what it had been. Luck. With every new person on the Island, the place became a better snack for the flying monsters.

Renity shook her head, still panting. "Come see."

Madelyn turned back into the hut, snatching up her cutlass. Once, she'd used a rapier, but the cutlass had grown on her. "Sorry, Miah. Sometimes you need an adventurer." She plucked up her brown leather hat with its long green feather and put it on. She tugged on the brim and winked.

Miah grunted.

Madelyn followed Renity out of the sweltering hut and down a stone street. People moved about, pursuing their own interests. Children played. A few people hauled bolts of cloth. When Madelyn ran past, though, they all watched.

They all knew who she was. And they knew if she was running with her blade, well, it might mean something important.

And Madelyn knew them all. She'd saved every single one of them by bringing them here. And with a little prodding, she'd spent time with them, too. There was Benton, a thin man from the southern nation of Ebhold. He'd lost his fields to the drought. There was Karin, a woman whose three sons served in the military, leaving her alone. Beskin and Drevo, twin boys, wrestled with each other like they always did. Ellene watched them, clutching her favorite doll.

Miah could yell at her all he wanted. She knew her people as well as he knew his metal. This was home, and she was determined to make sure anyone could stay here if they needed.

Madelyn and Renity dashed past the homes of the village and out to the fields. The entire Island had a flat top. Once outside the village itself, you could see to the rim. Green plants sprouted all over the fields. Grandma had suggested an apple orchard on one end of the Island, but those trees would take much longer to grow.

Madelyn was supposed to be learning about herbs from Essica, but she had no clue what plants she raced past now. Sugar beets? Strawberries? Maybe they were growing eggplants. They all looked about the same at this point. But did it really matter as long as the plants grew?

She shook her head. There wasn't time for this. She was already sweaty from the forge. Her new corset didn't breathe or bend nearly as much as her old one, either. It was a pain. She'd have to switch back to her old one. She didn't overheat nearly so fast in that one.

People working the fields stood up and brushed the dirt from their hands. They paused to watch as Renity and Madelyn raced by.

Finally, they reached the edge of the Island. The stone fell away. Below swirled the mists that swaddled the mountain range. Here and there, rocky peaks poked out of the clouds. The sun shone to Madelyn's left, descending for the day. A halo of floating stones encircled the Island. Not enough boulders circled here to block much of Madelyn's vision, though.

Gasping, she asked, "Where?"

Renity bent over, her hands on her knees. She flung a hand. "Look."

Madelyn squinted into the blue sky. Finally, she spotted a fleck on the horizon. "How did you spot that?"

"I've got good eyes."

"But you're way older than me."

Renity reached over to whack Madelyn, but she dodged.

"You're right, though. There's something out there. And it doesn't look like a dragon."

"But what else would be that big in the sky? It's not a pigeon!"

Madelyn shook her head. "You're right." She stared off into the distance, still panting. "Well, I'm glad it's still far away. I can hardly breathe after that run!"

"I had to run it twice!" Renity gulped air.

"You're more used to running. Being chased by boys."

Renity gave her a sideways glare. "You're nuts."

Madelyn kept her eyes on the far-off object. A dark feeling coiled around up in her gut. "What could it be?"

"That's what I asked."

"Well, I'm just as clueless."

They watched the sky. The sun sank. Two of the boulders in the halo clattered against each other. The breeze cooled the sweat on Madelyn's forehead.

"Is that . . . Is that a boat?" Madelyn asked.

Renity squinted. "Maybe? Who ever heard of a flying boat?"

"Who ever heard of a floating Island?" Madelyn tilted her head. "Maybe it's more fae? More people like me?"

Renity took her hand. "There's no one like you."

"Oh, shush. You know what I meant." The dark feeling pressed down on her. "A skyship? Maybe that's a thing. Look. It looks like the boat's hanging from something. Balloons, maybe?"

Her friend nodded. "So now what?"

The breeze shifted direction, blowing right into Madelyn's face. Her long dark hair fluttered behind her.

"Whoa," she said. "Look."

The boat in the distance grew, and grew quickly. It headed straight toward the Island now.

"Is that a good thing?" Renity asked.

And as she asked, a second boat appeared next to the first. And then another.

Soon, seven skyships sailed directly toward the Island.

And the dark feeling in Madelyn's gut grew darker.

CHAPTER TWO

The cold wind blew into their faces. The ships in the distance grew larger, from specks to the size of a fingernail to the size of a finger. Madelyn's heart beat faster.

"What should we do?" Renity asked.

Madelyn shook her head. "I wish Grandma was here."

"She's not. You're in charge. It's your Island, sis. What do we do?"

Madelyn bunched up the edge of her blouse, worrying the hem between her fingers. Whoever was out there could be friendly. If they were, having skyships like that could be useful for bringing supplies up to the Island. But what if they weren't friendly?

She had her cutlass. She could face off against a lot of people, but how many people would be on seven ships? And wherever they were from, it was beyond any place Madelyn had heard of. Who knew what other surprises they might bring?

Madelyn nodded. "We need to get Peter."

"Peter?" Renity huffed.

"He's from Fae. If he knows what these skyships are, it'll help. And if he doesn't, then at least we know they're human, right?"

"You want me to run and find him, don't you?"

"Well, you're a better runner, sis." Madelyn offered a quick grin. "You always were."

"I'm better than you at everything," Renity said.

"Except lifting rocks."

"All right. You win that one." Renity dashed off with another sigh.

Madelyn kept watch. One hand moved to the hilt of her cutlass at her side. What would happen if they weren't good people, whoever they were? Maybe she should have organized some way to defend the Island. But who could have ever guessed they'd be in danger here? No one from the surface could get to them. Humans couldn't fly!

But could fae?

She, Peter, and Grandma were the only fae she knew. The rest of the fae were on the other side of the Bridge, wherever that was. Grandma might know, but she wasn't telling. Madelyn had been carried over when she was only a baby, and Peter had stumbled over accidentally.

But if Peter stumbled across accidentally, anyone could, couldn't they?

The skyships continued to grow. Now Madelyn could see that they hung from huge faded red bags that were stuffed with strange shapes. Something floated there, suspending them in the air. Huge sails extended from the sides of the ships, almost like gigantic fins. The sails puffed under a strong wind.

But there was something wrong with the ships, too. One of them tilted sideways. Even from this distance, they looked ramshackle, as if cobbled together from other boats that weren't quite all the same size.

Ahead, the sun bent toward the horizon, turning the afternoon into early evening.

Running feet skidded to a stop behind her. Peter gasped out, "Sound the alarm."

"What alarm?" Madelyn asked, turning.

"Those're raiders. Fae raiders. I recognize the ships."

Madelyn's eyebrows knit together as she considered. Peter had faced down dragons for her and the Island, but she'd never heard fear in his voice before. "Are you sure? They could be refugees. Look at them. They look shabby."

"Course they're shabby! They don't have Houses. They're the ones who got kicked out."

"Weren't you kicked out?"

"I ran. I didn't take up piracy." Peter shook his head. "You gotta call the alarm. Get people who can fight. They're coming this way, and they're going to take whatever they want if we don't stop them first." He grabbed Madelyn's shoulders. "We don't have time to play. They're coming fast. They've seen the Island."

She looked into his eyes. She nodded. "Run back. Grab whoever you can. Miah. Anyone who can fight. Tell Essica we might need her help if someone gets wounded."

He nodded and ran without complaining.

That dark feeling threatened to overwhelm Madelyn as she turned back toward the skyships. Still, they floated closer, closer. Now they were the size of her hand and growing bigger by the second.

If Peter was right . . .

Grandma could do amazing things with stone. Peter could decompose things with a thought.

Madelyn was just learning what she could do herself as a half-fae. Even so, she could handle so much more than a normal person.

And if those were seven skyships full of fae? What could kinds of things could they do? There were thirteen Houses. Peter had been teaching her whatever he could, but they were both so busy, and she didn't expect to have to remember any of it. When would she ever encounter other fae?

Well, apparently right now.

Renity jogged back. "Are we done running back and forth?" she asked, panting. She'd strapped a rapier to her side.

"You don't know how to handle that sword."

"I can handle it better than you ever could." She hunched over, her hands on her knees, catching her breath. "Seriously. We gotta find some way to not have to run back and forth. It's gonna kill me if we keep this up."

"Peter raising the alarm?"

"What alarm?" Renity swallowed and straightened up. "Maybe we need one of those, too. But he's getting people moving, yeah. Miah's organizing them, arming anyone who can handle them-

17

selves. That last batch of refugees you brought in had a bruiser. He doesn't talk, but he's huge."

"Yeah. He was from up north. Gaershir, I think his name was. Said there was flooding."

"Oh, great. We've got refugees from Ebhold to the south, and now a refugee from up north? I don't even know what that place's called."

"Tell me about it." Madelyn shook her head.

Peter rushed up behind them.

"You might want a weapon," Madelyn said.

"Yeah, sure. I'd just stab myself with it. That the new bodice you've been messing with?"

"Hey! You're not supposed to know about that!"

Peter grinned through the dirt smudges that eternally marred his face. "Maybe not, but I do. It looks good on you."

Madelyn felt warmth on her cheeks. "We don't have time for that."

"You never have time for that."

Renity whacked him.

"Hey!"

"Someone has to do it, since Grandma isn't here."

He rubbed the back of his head. "You're not very nice."

"Not supposed to be. I gotta watch out for Madelyn." Renity put her hands on her hips and pushed her chin toward him. "If you want to mess with her, you'll have to get through me."

"You know I could just rust anything you'd throw at me."

"Oh, I think I'd be fine."

A small group of men ambled over the fields toward them. Miah led the way. He held a pair of large iron hammers. He winked as Madelyn eyed them. "You told me iron hurt anyone fae. I figured if Peter's right—"

"If?" Peter asked.

Miah ignored him. "If Peter's right and these are fae raiders, well, iron hammers should help us. If I'd known fae might threaten us, I might have been putting together more. After what those iron shackles did to you, imagine what would happen if one of these little boys hit you. Or them, I mean."

"We still don't know they're enemies," Madelyn said. "They might be refugees just like us."

"Better to be prepared in case they're not," Miah said.

"Listen to the blacksmith," Peter said, edging away from the hammer.

"Don't trust Peter," Miah said.

"Fine. Don't listen to the blacksmith," Peter said.

Madelyn rolled her eyes and looked at the other men.

A tall, hulking man with no hair grinned at her.

"Gaershir?" Madelyn asked.

He cracked his knuckles and nodded.

"I'm glad to be here," said another man. He was thin, wiry, and crouched low to the ground, so Madelyn couldn't tell how tall he actually was. "I was starting to get bored on this peaceful little Island of ours. I'm not good for much other than stabbing people."

Madelyn blinked.

"But no one up here needed stabbing, till now. I'm Burbin, my lady." He offered a shallow bow. "I worked for one of the Ebhold lords before he decided I knew too much."

Gaershir patted him on the back.

Burbin gave him a side-eye.

Gaershir laughed.

Madelyn glanced toward the village. "Is anyone else coming?"

Miah shook his head. "No one else really knows how to fight. Not well, at least. Some of the men are trying to set up a perimeter around the village to protect the children. There's women in that line too. But the most any of them have ever faced is a barroom brawl. I figured it'd be better if a few of us did whatever we could here."

Madelyn nodded, looking back to the skyships. They were so close now. "Well, they'll have to land or something. If we can keep them on their ships, or if they toss over lines and we just don't let them over, it'll be like fighting in a hallway. They can only send over one person at a time, right?"

Miah nodded. "Seems like a good strategy to me."

"I'd still feel better with more people."

"Well, maybe that's something we'll have to get ready for next time."

Madelyn sighed. "You're right. I don't like it, though."

"Good." Miah gave a grim smile as he watched the skyships' approach. "If you wanted to arm people, if you wanted to organize an army, I probably wouldn't want to help you. I'm not looking to start a war with anyone. Just live peacefully."

"Well. At least there's that." Madelyn drew her cutlass. "Everyone ready for whatever's coming?"

The small group spread out a little, drawing their various weapons. Burbin held two wicked daggers.

Renity stood at Madelyn's right and Peter at her left.

The skyships reached the halo of boulders and clattered through. Now Madelyn could see that the red bags above the ships were full of boulders. She shook her head. It was a good idea. A way to use her abilities to lift up more things at once. She'd have to remember that.

Depending what happened here.

That dark feeling coiled around her chest, her stomach, and even around her arms now. The wind kept shoving into her face.

The ships turned in the wind, showing the Island their sides. On the decks, men and women faced the Island. They watched Madelyn and the others. The sail wings flattened against the sides of the boats, letting them come even closer.

Madelyn and her friends could only watch and wait.

And then a voice bellowed from the skyships. "What're you waiting for? Lines away!"

The forms on the deck grabbed ropes and swung toward the Island.

CHAPTER THREE

S cores of men and women swung from their skyships toward the Island. They wore brightly-colored coats and the tight pants of sailors. Some held blades in their free hands. Others had weapons strapped to their sides. Others didn't seem to have any weapons at all. They all screamed as they swung across. Wordless yells filled Madelyn's ears, and thoughts raced through her mind faster than she could blink.

Nope. These weren't helpless refugees. Peter was right. Swinging over like that? These were raiders. Time to protect the Island.

Protect it from fae. From people like her. People who could construct skyships. People who might be able to do things like Peter. Maybe other things, too. Who knew what fae could do? Not her. All she could do was float rocks and fight with a sword.

And then she shook herself. She was Madelyn of the Sky, and she had a cutlass in her hand. This was where she shone. She shouted, "Looks like the odds are twenty to one or so." She tugged the brim of her hat. "Too bad for them!"

Burbin and Gaershir roared behind her. Miah bellowed. Renity screamed. Peter rolled his eyes.

"Peter. Decay their lines!" she ordered.

"On it!" He concentrated. The raiders swinging toward him lost their grip and plummeted through the air. Then the next two fell. They landed heavily on the ground near Madelyn. She kicked them hard on their heads. They slumped down, unconscious.

"Good! Keep it up!"

"They're coming too fast!" Peter said. "I can't get them all!"

Madelyn didn't reply. She rushed forward to meet the raiders where they'd land. Another pirate swung toward her. She spun her cutlass.

The man released his line while he was still in the air and kicked toward her. She sidestepped and let him fly into her cutlass. He fell to the ground, grabbing his wounded leg.

The next person landed on the Island. She kicked him. He fell off the edge.

Twenty to one. No problem at this rate. Madelyn glanced around to see how the others were doing.

Gaershir grinned like an idiot. He punched every raider who landed near him. They collapsed as quickly as he touched them. He laughed.

Burbin spun around Gaershir, protecting his back. His daggers flashed in the early evening light. He dodged every time Gaershir turned, as if they'd practiced fighting together for years. "This is too easy!" he crowed.

"Shouldn't say that," Peter grunted. "It's asking for trouble." He'd backed away from the edge of the Island. Too many raiders had crossed already for him to do much good there. Instead, he flung his hands out, turning blades to rust or decaying the very ground beneath the pirates, shaking their footing.

Miah spun his hammers, pummeling anyone within range. A little pile of pirates lay on the ground near him. Each had marks of blackened skin. The blacksmith snarled as he fought.

Renity danced through the raiders. Her lips pressed together in concentration, and her rapier darted here and there. She stabbed a man's leg so he fell. She dodged a slice and lunged in to pierce another pirate's arm.

And then Madelyn noticed: Most of the raiders weren't stopping to fight. Most pushed past their small band of defenders and rushed inland. Madelyn and the others weren't holding back the flood. They were hardly doing anything worthwhile, really. And those by the village, would they be able to fight back at all?

Madelyn kept fighting, but now she searched the crowd for a captain, a first mate, someone who might be in charge. Someone whose defeat could end the battle.

Then a strange sound rose up over the grunts and the clangs and the cries of battle.

Was that laughter?

Who was laughing?

Renity? Why would Renity be laughing?

And someone else was singing!

Renity still danced around the pirates, but now someone danced with her. A tall, thin man with tight pants and an open dark vest. He sang to the tune of his movements—some sort of shanty, though Madelyn didn't catch the words. He moved to parry her next thrust. His moves were timed perfectly with hers.

Renity was enjoying this? Her look of concentration was gone. She grinned as if this were a fantastic game. As their blades met again, she held her attack. He held his defense. They pushed against one another, and as they did, their faces drew closer and closer. He kissed her.

She kissed him back.

"Renity!" Madelyn yelped.

Her friend didn't notice. Instead, the kiss deepened. The pirate stepped away. Renity followed after him. He offered his hand. She took it.

The two dashed inland, hand in hand.

A pirate almost ran Madelyn through. She needed to pay attention to her own fight. But what had happened to her friend, her sister? How could she just kiss a pirate? Renity didn't have time for men. And now she was running off with some raider?

None of the pirates were trying to kiss Madelyn! Good thing, too. It wasn't polite to stab someone while they made kissy faces at you.

In frustration, she stabbed another pirate in the shoulder. He spun away and slipped on the loose stone near the edge of the Island, falling to the ground.

Nearby, Peter shook his head. "I don't think we're doing any good."

And then a pirate punched him in the side of

the head. "Ow," he said as he fell slobbering to the ground.

"Hey! I like him!" Madelyn shouted as she lunged at the pirate who'd done the deed.

No, she didn't like him. She really didn't. Peter was annoying. So none of that, thank you. Besides, there were pirates to stab.

Well. Two down. Renity racing off with a pirate, and Peter down with a blow to the head. At least the others were still fighting, right?

A rain of stones suddenly pelted Miah. He batted against them with his hammers, but they were too many. He stumbled as they struck him over and over again. He slipped to his knees. Another pirate tried to close in, but Miah rose again with a roar. He charged. The raider fell as Miah's hammer impacted his side. More stones fell. And more.

Miah fell again. He stumbled upright, only to take a knee. He groaned. He fell over. A pile of rocks soon covered his legs.

A rain of stones. Something Madelyn could do. If she had thought about it. If she could control what she did better.

But no. All she could do was float stones and fight with a blade.

Well. She'd better get fighting.

Even as she plunged into the battle again, she saw Gaershir. The big fellow had been mobbed. Six pirates all tackled him. He swung his fists. One of the raiders fell, cradling his stomach. Another flew backward.

Three more joined the tackle.

The northerner fell back against the onslaught into a tangle of arms and legs.

Burbin danced away, his daggers still shining in the light. "No, no, no," he said as a line of raiders formed up around him. "I don't like that. No, not at all."

One of the raiders stepped forward. "Neither do I. Go to sleep."

Burbin's face drooped. His daggers clattered to the ground. He fell over, snoring.

So Madelyn was the last one left. And what tricks would these fae attempt on her? More stone rain? Sleep? Someone trying to make kissy-face with her?

She glanced down at Peter as the thought flitted through her mind. Why would she look at him?

She shook herself again.

And then a woman stood near her. She held no weapons in her hands. She tilted her head. "It'd be smarter to let us grow where we will," she hissed.

"This is my Island," Madelyn snapped back. "Go home."

"Ah, we'd prefer familiar fields. But since we're here now, and you're in our way . . ." She flicked her fingers toward Madelyn.

The ground shifted. So, she was going to make her trip by wearing away the stone? Peter knew that trick too. Madelyn tried stepping aside calmly and nearly landed on her face.

Vines had grown up from the rock. Thorny tendrils wrapped around her ankles.

"Hey!" she shouted. "That's not fair!"

But the pirate turned her back and started moving toward the village.

That was it? They weren't even going to knock her out? They were going to treat her like she was nothing?

She wasn't nothing.

She was Madelyn of the Sky. She wasn't going to let them take her Island. She wasn't going to let them hurt her people!

She turned her cutlass on the vine. The blade bit into the thick skin of the tendril. She hacked at it again. Again! There wasn't time for this. She shouldn't have to fight some stupid vine. She should be fighting pirates!

30

With a grunt, she finally sliced through the plant and picked herself up off the ground. She flourished her cutlass, just to make herself feel a little better.

Bruises covered Miah's face, but he looked like he was breathing. Burbin slept. Gaershir lay under a pile of pirates. Renity was nowhere in sight. Peter lay on the ground where he'd been knocked out. Other than the pirates holding Gaershir down, though, there didn't seem to be any raiders here. They'd left their boats behind.

Madelyn rushed to Peter and knelt at his side, seeing how badly hurt he was.

Someone's boots crunched the gravel near her. She shot to her feet, cutlass in hand.

A tall man with a striking dark beard faced her. A long red coat hung from his shoulders. He held a rapier. "Aye, miss. You fight well, but you can't hold back the tide. Not when I call that tide."

She held her cutlass up in a guarded position. "Who're you?"

"I'm Captain Carangth. And whatever this Island holds is mine now. Unless you think you can face me?" He grinned. "I'm the best swordsman of seven Houses. I don't think you stand a chance, miss."

CHAPTER FOUR

M adelyn let the tip of her cutlass droop. "You're the best swordsman in seven Houses?" She looked the bearded man up and down. "Only seven Houses?" Madelyn felt her mouth quirk up into a smirk. "I thought there were thirteen Houses. I guess you're not that good, then."

Captain Carangth tilted his head ever so slightly. "You've got some fire in you, miss. I'd hate to put any of that out. Let us pass, and I'll see that you're not harmed."

"Let you pass? Let you trespass on my Island? I don't think so." She flicked her cutlass back up, prepared for any attack.

Here she was, fighting one man. Just one. There weren't any dragons to worry about. She didn't have to protect any refugees or any prince. It was just the two of them. Madelyn knew how to do two things: float rocks and fight with a blade. And this was her home turf.

A full smile bloomed on her face. "Why don't we make a deal."

"A deal? Not a good idea to deal with fae. Or pirates." Carangth's grin matched her own. "You never know when they might renege." His rapier snapped out toward her.

Madelyn blocked it without a thought. He was testing her. She had no problem proving she could face him. "Hear me out. I could kill you right now." She flicked her cutlass just so, right past his guard, and tore the fabric of his sleeve.

He lifted an eyebrow. "You're fast, miss. I'll give you that."

"Exactly. So here's the deal. You and me, we fight. You with your rapier, me with my cutlass. No tricks. You don't pull any of your little fae magic. None of your crew steps in. None of my people helps me. If you win, you get the Island. If I win, you and your crews shove off." Madelyn's grin grew.

She knew she could win this.

Of course she could.

He dropped his guard. "Now see here. I'm an honorable man. I make sure my men don't bother anyone unless they get in our way. And I don't like striking anyone who doesn't deserve it. We all got enough of that. You're only protecting what's yours. I understand that. I respect it. There's only one thing we need here. Well, and some supplies."

"Oh?" Now Madelyn raised an eyebrow.

"Enough of that. This seemed like good harbor. But you're standing between me and what we need." Carangth saluted her. "You've provided a fine distraction. This farce is done." His blade whistled through the air toward Madelyn's face.

Her blade met it. She lifted her sword and sliced toward him.

He stepped back out of her reach.

"I fought with the rapier for a long time. I know what it can do and what it can't do." Madelyn smirked and pressed her attack. "I know how much stress a blade can handle. Someone gave me their cutlass, and, well, I haven't gone back."

"The rapier is the blade of a gentleman." Carangth gave ground, stepping back once, twice under Madelyn's furious assault.

"You're no gentleman," she said.

"You won't goad me into hurting you. I don't hurt children."

Madelyn struck again and again. "I'm not a child!" She huffed.

"You look it to me." He stopped her cutlass with his blade and shoved off. "Just a little girl."

Madelyn narrowed her eyes. "Oh. I see. You're goading me! You're letting me win with the sword but trying to strike me with your words? That some kind of fae trick?"

"Well, it was worth a try, wasn't it?" His rapier danced around her now. This time Madelyn retreated a step. "A gentleman uses many tactics."

"A pirate gentleman? You just can't decide what you want to be. I suppose you're just raiding to support a family back home. Ten little children and an innocent woman all waiting for papa to get back. What would they do if they found out you couldn't even defeat a little girl?" Madelyn grinned, parrying every attack.

Carangth lunged. Madelyn was ready. She turned out of the way, letting the rapier snag the edge of her skirt. She slammed down on his blade with the edge of her own with all her strength. Sparks flew. His rapier bent and cracked. A useless metal chunk fell to the ground. He was left holding a stub of a rapier.

"I told you I knew how rapiers work. They're thin. They give so much. Useful in battle." Madelyn winked. "But if they bend too far, well, they just can't handle the pressure."

Carangth regarded his hilt and nodded. "All right. You know how to fight, miss; I'll give you that, too. Not what we expected of humans." He tossed the hilt over the edge of the Island. He regarded her. "How did you know there are thirteen Houses?"

"What do you mean?"

"I told you I was the best swordsman in seven Houses. And you were full of bravado, like a good pirate. And what did you say? It was sad I wasn't the best swordsman in thirteen Houses. How would a human know that?" He tilted his head, his eyes still on her. "You are curious, aren't you?"

He had no weapon. So why was Madelyn suddenly scared?

"We came here hungry. We've been far too long since resupplying. We didn't come for just food, though. Maybe what we really wanted is standing right in front of me. You're not just one of the residents of this Island, are you? Oh, we've heard the stories. Of a human who's something more. Something far more." He stepped toward her.

Madelyn scrambled backward. "Stay back!"

"Stories of a woman with amazing powers. Someone who raised an Island into the sky. There's no human who could ever do such a thing. But we have legends on the other side of the Bridge. Hushed whispers from House Stone." He stepped toward her again.

Madelyn raised her cutlass. "I'm warning you!"

"We need someone like that. Someone who doesn't belong here and doesn't belong there. And now I've found you, haven't I? Madelyn of the Sky, they call you?" He lifted his right hand. Though it was empty, Madelyn flinched. "Well. Now the game must end, sadly." He twisted his wrist. A blade sprang from the sleeve of his coat. Not long, barely more than a dagger, but enough.

Like lightning, he struck forward, past Madelyn's guard, plunging the dagger toward her stomach.

The red, red sun touched the horizon in the distance. The wind pushed into Madelyn's face. Carangth swallowed. "I'm sorry, miss. Truly I am. But I need you, and I suspect the only way to get you onto my boat is to make it so you can't fight back." He looked down at the blade in his hand. He frowned.

Madelyn grinned. "Stone bodice. Been working on what else I can do with stone. Doesn't breathe much, but it pays when someone tries to stab you." She spun her cutlass up, shoving the dagger away.

He turned the blade right toward her again. He was so close. She blocked the blade. It came in again. She missed. It scraped against her bodice. Sparks flew. He grunted as he pushed against her. He kicked her.

His boot landed against her knee. She fell to the ground.

He panted over her, trying to catch his breath. "Yes, miss. Well fought. But now you belong to me." He placed the blade under her chin, against her throat.

"You cheated," she said.

"Well, I am a pirate. In case you missed that."

"A pretty sorry one. You almost let a girl beat you."

"I thought you weren't a girl?" He raised an eyebrow. "And if you're Madelyn of the Sky, well, you're good enough for a fight."

"You sure it's over?"

He huffed a laugh. "I've got my blade against your throat. Aye, I think it's done."

She closed her eyes. Fast as she ever had done before, she spoke to the stone under her fingers. It listened and thought her idea a fantastic prank.

The ground under the captain's left foot shot skyward. He stumbled.

Madelyn kicked him in the knee as hard as she could.

He fell in a heap. He cursed in languages Madelyn had never heard of. His blade swung wide, not even scratching her.

She scrambled to her feet and sprinted away.

The captain screamed out, "Get her! We need that wench!"

CHAPTER FIVE

Madelyn dashed across the open fields. Green growing things pushed against her ankles. She yelped and jumped. No, they weren't vines grown by some fae pirate. Just what was supposed to be here. Crops. She was safe. For now.

Captain Carangth bellowed after her but didn't chase. No one chased her. No one seemed to be in the fields now.

The village. All the pirates who had raced past had been trying to get to the village. What was happening there? What was happening to the people she'd saved?

This was supposed to be a safe place. No one was supposed to get to them here. She'd promised them. A haven. A home where no one would hurt them again. If she couldn't keep that promise, what good was she?

No. She didn't know there were pirates who had flying ships. How could she have known that? She didn't even know what fae were a month ago. And she still didn't know. Not really. This wasn't her fault.

But she'd fix it. That's what she did, right? Madelyn of the Sky would protect her people. She had stood against Kenevir's army and had turned them back with the help of friends. If she could face off against an entire army, she could handle a few boats of pirates. Maybe she could wake Peter and go down to bring dragons up here? It had worked against the army, after all.

But they probably didn't have time. By the time they got down to the dragon caves, the pirates could be gone. Plus, she was running away from where Peter had fallen. Even if she went back, would she be able to wake Peter up?

She stumbled. What would happen if she couldn't wake Peter up?

No. She'd wake Peter up. It would be fine. Of course it'd be fine.

She glanced back at the captain who still stood near the edge of the Island. His ships hung in the sky behind him. From this distance, Madelyn couldn't see his expression, but she felt his eyes on her.

Well. There was no place to hide on the Island. Not really. They didn't think they'd need anything like that up here.

Madelyn finally reached the edge of town. Her steps took her around the first building, out of sight of the captain. She took a moment to regather herself without his eyes on her. She tried to slow her breathing.

Laughter sounded from the town ahead of her. Madelyn shivered. Why would there be laughter?

She crept toward the next building.

She almost fell into the pit. She barely kept herself from yelping in surprise. That hadn't been there earlier today.

A few men stood at the bottom of the pit. "Madelyn!" hissed one. Travin. His name was Travin. A young man, just a few years older than she was. He'd come from Ebhold when his family had been captured by bandits.

Madelyn mentally rolled her eyes at herself. Yes, she knew her people, but that wasn't the point right now. She crouched at the edge of the pit. "What happened?"

"The pirates! We were going to fight them when this hole opened up. We fell in! Give us a hand up." He clenched his fists. "We're not letting them take our home."

Madelyn grinned. "Good!" She reached down.

Travin jumped but missed her fingers. She lay on the ground to reach lower. Still he couldn't reach. The other men took turns. They boosted each other up. Still not enough.

"Think you can make stairs out of the sides of the pit?" another man asked.

"I can try," she answered. She set her fingertips on the stone along the edge of the pit and closed her eyes. Sparks flowed from her heart, warming her shoulder, her elbow, her knuckles, every joint. She didn't hurry this time. The stone greeted her with joy.

Madelyn asked if the stone would be interested in helping the men trapped below.

The stone really didn't care about them. They never talked to rocks like she did.

But would the stone please do her this favor? Flowing and reforming could be so much fun, like stretching your back. And the shape of stairs was so comfortable.

The stone here had already been reshaped. Someone else had talked to it! It was good to hear another voice. And being a pit was quite a bit different. It had never been in this shape before.

Madelyn grunted in frustration. Please? For her? She'd taught the stone how to fly in the first place.

Oh, yes, and that was joy as well. But for now, it was content, thank you.

She jerked her fingers away. "It won't listen to me," she said. "One of the fae talks to stone, too, and they're better at convincing it to listen than I am." Someone was better at talking to stone than her.

She didn't have time to think about it now. She tried to tuck the thought away, but it nibbled at the edge of her mind.

"So we're stuck down here?" the man who'd suggested making stairs asked.

"I'm sorry. For now." Madelyn stood. What was this? She couldn't even rescue of a few of the people who depended on her. "I won't leave you there for long, though. Don't worry. I want your help getting these guys off our Island."

The men nodded with resolve. "We'll be waiting."

Madelyn swallowed as she looked down at them. If she couldn't even get rocks to listen to her, what was she supposed to do?

Well, for now, she should get a look at what was happening in the village, shouldn't she?

She looked at the building beside her. It was someone's home. Travin's, maybe? Grandma had shaped it a few weeks ago. But Madelyn needed to get higher to see what was going on. Higher than just a house. The next building over stood taller. It was meant to be a storehouse for any crops that came from the fields, plenty tall to handle however much food they could grow. Grandma had made it look like stone bricks. Easy to climb.

That was good. Renity was the climber, not Madelyn, but she should be able to handle this. She glanced around. No one in sight. Good. She dashed over to the storehouse. With a grunt, she hauled herself up to top. She lay on the flat roof and looked over the village.

She sighed. What was she supposed to do?

Pits yawned in many places. People called out to one another. Some around the village were bound by vines. Others slept on the ground. A few others held hands or kissed each other. Stone had flowed around Essica, their wisewoman, holding her feet fast. Everyone seemed incapacitated in some way, but at least, as far as she could tell, no one seemed seriously hurt.

Laughter. Familiar laughter.

Renity's laughter!

Below, a familiar shape walked out of the storehouse. He scowled. Renity's fingers still entwined with his.

"Come on, Rapsod. I want to introduce you to my friends." She grinned at him. "You'd like them. They're fun like you."

"Are you sure this is all the food you have?" the fae asked, ignoring what Renity said.

"Look, I'm not going to lie to you. I don't like lying. This is all the food we have right now. There's a reason we're growing more!" She giggled. "Oh, Rapsod, don't look at me like that." A little of her voice's usual edge returned. "I'm all you need anyway."

He turned to look at her. "Right." He shook his head with a sigh.

"I'll dance with you. And that's all you need. Someone who'll dance with you without ever looking back."

He didn't turn away from her. "Listen. I cast a spell on you. It's what I do. It's how I fight. And now

46

you're still under that spell. You think you're in love. You're not. You're pretty. There's something about humans, and you've got a lot of it. And sure, that dance was something else. But you don't have what we need."

"They do."

Madelyn flattened herself against the roof as much as she could. Captain Carangth limped into town.

The pirate who had danced with Renity, Rapsod, straightened. "Captain."

"She's here. Madelyn of the Sky. She's the key to us getting home. She's the one we need. Tear this place apart until you find her."

"They do—"

CHAPTER SIX

M adelyn cursed. Quietly. And then she wrinkled her nose. Grandma always whacked her upside the head when she cursed.

The pirates wanted her? What for? Should she just give herself up? Trade herself to them so they would leave the Island?

No. That wouldn't help. Grandma still hadn't learned how to float stone this large. She could lift others to the Island, but she couldn't keep the entire thing afloat. If Madelyn left, the entire Island would crash to the ground. Not right away. Maybe they'd be able to get everyone to safety. But then all the refugees would be without a home again, and then the conflict with Kenevir would probably start all over again.

So giving herself up wasn't an option.

She would have to find some other way to get rid of the pirates. And she would probably need help.

She couldn't get Travin or the others out of the pit. That probably meant all the other pits would be about as deep. Couldn't save any of them quickly, then. It had taken her too long to hack her legs free of the vines to be able to free too many people trapped that way before being discovered. Could she wake those who had fallen asleep? If she asked Renity for help, what would happen then?

So much for getting help. She was alone, the last defender of the Island. And it was her job to save it. All she had was her cutlass, which wouldn't do much good against so many pirates. She had her wits, which probably weren't worth much.

And she could float stone.

Madelyn narrowed her eyes, looking down on the captain, Rapsod, and Renity. Could she reach down through the Island and maybe just float them up and away?

No. That wouldn't work. They'd just step right off the rock and know that she was close. The worst that would happen would be some twisted ankles. She couldn't float the pirates off the Island.

But what if she could float their skyships away?

She looked back to where the skyships floated at the edge of the Island. They hung suspended from faded red tarps full of floating stones. If she convinced those stones to float higher, would that take away their boats? What would happen then?

It was worth trying. At least she'd be doing something.

Now she just had to figure out how to get to them. If she ran across the fields, everyone would be able to see her. She wished the mists of the hills below the Island would surge up and swaddle them all in fog, but that wasn't likely to happen. She hadn't mastered using her skills to burrow tunnels, either, which meant she couldn't go through the Island.

So she couldn't cross the Island. She couldn't go under it.

Madelyn looked up at the halo of boulders that surrounded the Island.

Apparently, she'd have to go over the Island.

She hoped no one would notice her. She spread her hand on part of the stone rooftop and asked if it'd like to rise up even higher.

That sounded like fun.

As quietly as she could, she convinced part of the stone to flow away, allowing a portion of the roof just large enough to hold her to separate. Soon it floated upward.

Madelyn crept so she could peek over the edge. Pirates scrambled around the village, looking down into pits, poking their heads into every building. Thankfully, they didn't look up. It was amazing how seldom people looked up. By now, the sky was darkening too. That helped.

She held her breath as the stone floated up, up, until it joined the halo of stones. Soon she was high enough she couldn't hear anything from down below. The crisp air was cold against her skin. She should have grabbed her cloak, but it had been warm near the forge. Besides, she had bigger things to worry about than her cloak.

Madelyn examined the boulders around her. Yes, here the rocks were close enough. She should be able to jump from one to another to another. Most of these she'd used to lift people or supplies to the Island. They hadn't wanted to meld together to form the Island itself, so she'd left them to orbit or to carry her back down whenever she needed to return to the ground. That meant most were wide enough to hold her with no problem.

At least, it should be that easy.

Madelyn looked at the jump from her stone to the next and took a deep breath. Yep. She could jump that far. Not a problem. All she had to do was make sure she didn't think about what would happen if she missed. Oh, she wished she could do more than make stones float.

She tugged the brim of her hat and locked her eyes onto the next stone. She ran as hard as she could in the little space.

With a grunt, she pushed off. Open air yawned below her. Her stomach seemed to fall, even as the rest of her stretched toward the next rock.

And then she landed, simple as that. Her heart thundered in her chest, but she'd made it.

Now she just had to do it again. And again. And again, until she made it to the pirate ships. Oh, and she had to do it fast enough that the raiders didn't realize she wasn't in the village after all.

Should be easy. Right.

Well, at least it meant she didn't have time to think about it. She jumped to the next stone and then the next. After more jumps, she lost track of how far she'd come. Maybe it was even fun, if she let herself forget what would happen if she missed a jump.

After far too long, she made it to the part of the halo that overlooked the pirate ships. All she had to do was land on top of one of the tarps holding the rocks above the boats and convince those rocks to rise higher. The pirates would notice one boat was getting away, and they'd all run back to their boats, afraid of being left behind.

At least that was the theory.

She gazed down at the seven boats all pulled up alongside the Island. Someone had lowered gangplanks from the ships to the ground. Some people gathered on the Island near those planks, but no one looked up.

Madelyn grinned. It was just one more jump from her current rock to the stones above the boat. No one had looked up yet. Twilight had set in, so it was even darker now.

She took a deep breath and jumped one last time.

She landed on the cloth tarp. No, it wasn't cloth at all, was it? It was stiffer and felt oddly smooth. Maybe it was coated with something to make it waterproof? Some sort of wax?

Well, as long as she could speak to the stone through it, it didn't really matter, did it? She drew her cutlass and cut through the tarp, just enough she could place her hand against the stone beneath. The sparks ran from her heart to her palm and out through her fingertips.

Hello.

Oh, this stone loved flying through the sky. It rejoiced in feeling the warmth of the sun and the cool of the air.

Well, don't you think you could fly even higher? Madelyn urged it. Perhaps you could touch the moon.

The stone had never considered that. Touch the moon? Was the moon made of stone? Maybe it could talk with its cousins so far above.

Madelyn suppressed a giggle. Well, if you want to touch the moon, why don't you try?

And the stones began to rise. The boat below groaned as it lifted suddenly. Voices shouted.

Madelyn leaped for one of the stones in the halo. Not a problem. She was safe, and the pirate ship lifted higher and higher. More shouts sounded. Angry shouts.

Good. Get on your other boats. Chase that ship down. Go catch it and leave!

Already, the fugitive ship had escaped the halo, flying higher and higher. They might never catch it, it was going so fast! Well, it was a pleasure speaking to stones already used to moving. They went so much quicker than her usual, sluggish stones!

Madelyn peeked over the edge of the rock she hid on. The pirates should be boarding their other boats, right?

"There!" The shout came as soon as she looked over the edge. The stone suddenly jerked and began floating down toward the Island.

Her heart thundered again. Someone had spotted her. How could someone speak to stone from so far away? Was it because she was half fae that she couldn't reach as far? Now what? Should she try speaking to the stone herself?

No. Last time she tried that, the stone had sided with the pirates.

Instead, she jumped to a nearby stone. If she could get farther away, maybe they wouldn't be able to chase her. She could find some other way to strike at the pirates and make them leave.

The next stone began to sink as soon as her feet touched it. She ran across it and jumped to another. She didn't even have time to feel afraid. Good thing, too.

"Captain!"

"I see her. Just get her down here. That's the one we need!"

"But *Debbie*—"

"We'll get her back. Right now, concentrate on the girl."

Madelyn sprinted. It was getting harder to breathe. This bodice really didn't give her enough room for panting. Another stone. Another. Was she getting ahead of them at all? Did she dare even look?

Maybe.

She skidded to a stop and flopped over on top of a rock. She slapped her hand down against its surface. Sparks ran from her heart to her fingertips.

Fly me, stone. Fly high!

The stone answered by lifting her higher. Higher.

If only she could get away, get out of range, then maybe the other fae wouldn't be able to yank her down again. Maybe she would be safe.

Finally, when she could no longer hear anything but the wind, Madelyn closed her eyes and set her forehead on the stone.

Everyone on the Island. They were trapped. The pirates were going to pillage any food they had. They were already dangerously low in stores. The drought meant there wasn't much in the way of supplies for them to purchase, and their own crops hadn't produced anything yet. And now that the raiders had lost a ship, well, that hadn't worked the way she'd intended. They were supposed to chase that boat and leave!

Some rescue that was.

She tapped her forehead against the stone. She had to think. There had to be something she could do. Something!

The stone jerked to a stop.

No. How could anyone reach that far?

The stone flowed over her hands, anchoring her to its surface. She tugged against it, but it wouldn't give. She shot sparks into it. How could you do this to me?

The stone answered that it thought maybe it would be fun to keep her close. For now, at least.

And then another boulder floated up from below. A thin figure stood atop it, swaddled in a huge cloak. "Not bad. You made me run. But no one runs as fast as I do." It was a girl? She sounded younger than Madelyn!

"Yeah, I don't run too fast. But we could race if you wanted," Madelyn called back. "You'd have to get the stone to let me go, though."

"I think you already lost the race. And now you're coming back with me. Captain Carangth says we need you to get home. And, well, these human lands are a bit scary. I'd like to go home."

And with that, their stones turned back toward the pirate skyships.

CHAPTER SEVEN

Madelyn tugged at her hands just a few times before giving up. She shot sparks into the stone. It ignored her pleading. She finally lay still, that dark feeling coiling all around her.

She'd failed.

The fae on the stone next to her lifted her face to the breeze, letting her long cloak billow behind her. She looked like she was maybe twelve years old.

Madelyn stuffed her dark feelings away as best she could. They wouldn't help her. She wasn't defeated. Not yet. Sure, she couldn't use her sword right now, and apparently speaking to stone wasn't that unusual, but there had to be something she could do. After all, she'd been in worse shape when she'd been captured and put in iron chains just a month ago.

Of course she'd get out of this. All she had to do was keep looking for ways to get out. And that started by finding out about who had captured her.

"How can you be a pirate when you're so young?" Madelyn asked.

The other form jumped but composed herself quickly. "I'm not too young to be a pirate. I'm almost thirty!"

Madelyn couldn't help laughing. "Thirty? You're younger than I am!"

"You humans age fast. It's sad. Part of what makes you so scary. When you age like that, you do things without thinking." She offered a sad smile.

"I'm not human," Madelyn grunted.

"Oh, that's right. Humans can't talk to stone, can they? But you're not exactly fae either." The smaller girl brought her stone alongside Madelyn's. "I'm Guri. What's your name?"

"Madelyn." She searched the fae's face. "Let me out. Please. I don't know what your captain wants with me, but this is my home."

"Sorry. Captain Carangth gives the orders over the fleet. I just take care of the ships, keep them flying. Wouldn't do any good to have them falling out of the sky." She reached over and patted Madelyn on the shoulder. "But don't worry. He's a good captain. Takes care of his crew. And unless he's keeping you for ransom, you're going to be part of the crew."

"This is my home. It's the only place I've ever belonged." She looked over at her Island.

Guri laughed. "Well, it's time for you to belong someplace else, then. Welcome to the fleet."

Their stones passed the tarps and came level with the deck of one of the skyships. Carangth waited there, his hands on his hips. His grin was wide. "There she is. Guri, well done, lass. Extra grog for you tonight."

"There isn't any grog left, Captain."

"Well, we'll pretend to give you extra grog, then." He laughed. "And there. Our treasure. Madelyn of the Sky."

"Treasure, Captain?" Guri squinted at him. "She's not crew?"

"She might be. Eventually. But she's our way home. And right now, that's what makes her special. More special than the Wicker Shovel from House Grave." His eyes shone in the dim light. "Release her, lass. Let her board the ship."

The stone flowed away from Madelyn's hands. She wiggled her fingers, using the moment to try and speak with the rock again.

It was quite content to talk with Guri, thank you. She was a lot of fun.

Well, she wasn't going to get away that way. All right, then.

Madelyn rose and stretched out her back. "You really think I'll come with you."

"If you come with us, we won't bother your little Island anymore." Carangth held out a hand to her. "Step lively, now. It's not good to keep a captain waiting."

She glanced back toward the Island. Her home. The place she had made, the place where her friends lived.

But they hadn't been strong enough to keep the pirates away, had they? If she kept fighting and the pirates stayed, what else would happen?

But if she left, the Island would fall. That's why she fought in the first place.

"I can't leave without speaking to the Island," Madelyn said. "If I go, it'll fall from the sky. My people need me."

Something shifted in Carangth's face. "You want to protect your crew." He nodded. "I respect that.

But I'm sorry, miss, I can't let you back there. You've caused us some trouble already, and I'd rather not lose you again." He considered. "What does your Island need?"

"I need to remind it to keep flying," she said.

"Guri?"

"Got it, Captain." Guri hopped off her stone and onto the deck. From there, she moved to the other side of the deck and down the gangplank to the Island. She returned a few moments later. "She'll be happy to fly now unless there's no one to hold up. You won't need to worry about it."

"You can do that?" Madelyn had a hard time catching her breath. "You won't need to keep reminding the stone? How did you do that?"

Guri shrugged. "It's what I do."

"Now, miss, we've done far more than is necessary. We've even protected your Island. We'll be shoving off as soon as you step over." Carangth extended his hand again.

Madelyn took a deep breath and tugged the brim of her hat. Her hand trembled as she lifted it and placed it in the captain's. She took the single step from the stone onto the deck.

The captain didn't move his eyes from hers as he ordered, "Prepare to make sail."

All around the deck, men and women burst into activity. Madelyn hadn't even noticed them before; she'd been so focused on the captain and Guri. The gangplank lifted from the Island. Someone blew a deep trumpet. Forms ran and jumped across to the skyships.

"When all's accounted for, we'll get our fugitive ship," the captain said to those on the deck. "Make ready."

"Aye, Captain!"

"You," he addressed Madelyn, "stay out of the way. I'll let you watch your Island as we shove off. No tricks. You're here now."

Her eyes darted. Could she jump across? She spotted the lines the pirates had used to swing to the Island. She could use one of those easily.

But so could Carangth or any of the others. She wouldn't get far.

The wind changed direction. The sails that extended from the sides of the ship puffed out. The deck creaked as the ship tilted ever so slightly. Men and women still ran toward the skyships, jumping across. They hauled themselves over the sides of the ship, climbing onto the deck and going about their business as if they did this all the time.

Someone was screaming.

A hand came over the side of the boat, lifting up a familiar face. Rapsod, the one who'd danced with Renity, soon stood on the deck. He wasn't smiling.

Madelyn moved to the rail that lined the deck. There, standing on the edge of the Island, yelled Renity. "Don't you dare dance with me and leave like that!"

Carangth stepped over and glanced down at her. "You really need to leave a wench like that at every port, don't you?"

"It's all I can do, Captain. It's why you took me on."

The captain looked at Rapsod. "So I did. It's a shame, though. She had some magic in her, didn't she?"

"She's human." Rapsod gazed back at Renity. "I've never known one before."

"Just another reason to get home before this place bewitches us." He patted Rapsod on the shoulder.

The last of the pirates boarded the other boats. They turned out of the halo of stones and tilted upward, pointing toward the moon. Madelyn watched her Island fade into darkness.

"Now, miss, I'll show you to your quarters." Carangth laid a heavy hand on her shoulder.

She allowed him to guide her across the deck to a bright red door. He swung it open to reveal a lavish room filled with artifacts she couldn't identify and a gigantic bed. A wide wooden table took up most of the room. Huge windows dominated the far wall, showing the sky ahead of the ship. "You'll be staying in my cabin for the duration, until we find out what we'll be doing with you. Make yourself comfortable. You may be here a while."

He shut the door behind him, leaving Madelyn alone and far from her home.

CHAPTER EIGHT

O utside the door, Madelyn heard the crew working. They thumped across the deck and called to each other. The wind whistled through the lines on the sails and the heavy cords that hung between the ship and the floating stones. Soon someone began singing in tune to that whistling, and another voice joined in.

The music felt so strange. It had a rhythmic drive but like nothing she'd heard before. The notes felt spicy somehow, like they had some sort of bite to them. They held a longing, too. It reminded her of the songs refugees sang of their homes.

Madelyn placed her hand against the door and listened. She tried to make out the words to the song, but the door muffled too much of the sound.

Were these the sounds of her mother's home? Is this what fae were? Peter hadn't said good things about fae, and her grandma still didn't tell her much. Just that fae couldn't lie, and they had to keep their promises. Be careful, though, Grandma said. Fae could twist and knot words better than an old woman twisted yarn.

Still, here were people like her. People who could do things. Guri could talk to stone. Madelyn could learn so much from her.

But these pirates weren't like her at all, were they? Guri said she was thirty years old. And she was already so much more powerful than Madelyn.

And it meant Madelyn wasn't so special, was she? The question returned to her, draping her in a dark mood. Before, she was the only one who could lift the Island. It made her special. So many people could handle blades. She'd been the only one who could float stones. But now what? She wished Peter was here to talk to. He was always annoying enough he distracted her.

The song faded as more people called out to each other. The captain roared something. Maybe they were catching up to the boat she'd sent toward the moon. Maybe they were going to reclaim it for themselves.

Finally, Madelyn turned back toward the huge room. It was grand, almost welcoming. Something felt off when she looked at the walls, though, as if the room was wider than the skyship, but not so much that it was noticeable at first glance. It smelled of pleasant oils.

A massive wooden table dominated the center of the room. No chairs stood around it. As Madelyn approached it, she noticed the surface looked wet. She placed her hand on it. It felt dry, but ripples flowed from her touch. They bounced against the other edges of the table and came back to her. After a moment, the ripples formed into a face which rose and floated above the table.

Peter's face.

Madelyn gasped and yanked her hand back. The ripples, and the face with them, faded.

She stepped carefully around the table. Lamps hung from the ceiling timbers. Each one burned a slightly different color. She reached up to touch one. As she did, it burned brighter, and the other lamps dimmed. When she removed her hand, they all returned to their previous brightness.

Paintings of upside-down lands hung on the walls. Trees grew down. The sun rose toward the horizon.

None of it made any sense.

Fatigue began to pull at her arms. She had fought for too long. She recognized the feeling. It wasn't the first time she'd had to fight impossible odds. It wasn't even the first time she'd been captured. Sure, she might be tired, but she'd find a way home. She had to.

Should she lie down? The bed was huge and inviting. It certainly looked more comfortable than her cot back at the Island.

No. This was a pirate ship. She couldn't sleep here.

But what if they kept her for a long time? Shouldn't she take care of herself, so when she got the chance, she could escape?

The ship leveled off. They must have caught up with the other boat. More shouting from outside. That meant whatever they were planning to do with her, it would be soon.

As if he'd been waiting for that thought, the captain swung the door open. Rapsod followed and shut the door behind him. Captain Carangth stepped to the table and tapped it. The ripples spread from his touch, bounced back and off the table, and formed a chair that rested on the ground. The captain sat. Rapsod stood behind him.

"Well, Madelyn of the Sky," the captain began, "I was going to ask what House you were, but I'd wager you're House Stone. Am I right?"

Madelyn faced him but remained silent.

"You spoke to the stone. You floated an Island. It's obvious."

She wrinkled her nose. "What House are you?"

"Ah, miss, I'm a pirate. No House will have me. But for now, I need you: a child of two worlds, neither fae nor human, but both. And that means you're the key to getting us home. Rapsod?"

The other man stepped forward. The table still stood between them, but Madelyn took a step away anyway.

Rapsod raised his hands. "Don't worry. I don't want to hurt you." He closed his eyes and hummed. Soon the hums turned into a tonal moaning. His voice rose and fell. Phrases ended with almost a sob.

And the music spoke to Madelyn.

They wanted to go home. That's all the pirates wanted. They needed supplies. They were hungry. That's why they had come to the Island. But this was such a strange world. The human world didn't work the way it was supposed to.

And then the song began to beg her.

Please, please, show us how to get home. We're lost. Take us to the Bridge. Tell us how to cross. That's all we're asking.

When had she started crying? She was crying for pirates?

Well, why shouldn't she? They were lost. She helped people find their homes. It's what she did. Refugees wanted to go home, and she helped them. She saved them. Why shouldn't she help these pirates? They weren't any worse.

Yes they were! They stole from the Island! They didn't ask for help. They'd kidnapped her!

But they hadn't killed anyone, had they?

Well, not that she saw. That didn't mean they didn't kill anyone. What if Peter never woke up? Look what they did to Renity!

And Madelyn argued with herself and with the song. Should she show mercy? Should she help them return?

Tears ran down Rapsod's cheeks. He didn't reach out to her. He didn't do anything other than sing. His voice bent and broke and rose again, moaning a terrible lament. He longed for the mysteries of his own land. He hungered to behold its wonders again. But now, now all was lost. They couldn't find their way home. All that was left was an emptiness in their hearts.

Madelyn found herself sobbing. She felt so bad for them. Sure, they did nasty things; sure they stole, but they were good people. Good pirates. And if they went home, they'd never bother her again. And they'd helped the Island, hadn't they? They didn't have to do that at all.

So what should she do?

No. That was the wrong question.

What was the right thing to do?

Because she should do the right thing. And the right thing was helping them find their way home. It was that simple, wasn't it?

"I'll help you," she said. "I'll help you get home. Just don't ever raid human lands again."

"Ah," Carangth said, "we don't want to ever come back if we don't have to. Just get us home."

Rapsod kept singing, lost in the wordless music. He swayed on his feet in time to the strange rhythms.

"What do you need me to do?"

"Take us to the Bridge so we can cross back," the captain said.

73

"Take you to the Bridge? Back to Fae? I don't know where that is." Madelyn shook her head. "I've never known how to get there."

"You must! You're a daughter of two worlds. Less than fae, less than human, more than both. You point like a compass to the Bridge no matter where you are."

"What're you talking about?"

"You're not the first half-human to come from our lands, though it's been a long time, miss. And the stories say that no matter how far you wander from the Bridge, if you have blood of human and blood of fae, you can find your way back." The captain rose from his chair. "Take us home. You're the only one who can."

Madelyn shook her head, tears still streaming from her face. "I don't know how!"

"A direction. A heading. Anything!"

She only shook her head again.

Rapsod's song faded in a long, unresolved note. He shuddered. "Captain, I need to go," he said, his voice quiet.

"Go. Tell Stuhi to pick a direction and blow the winds. We at least can be moving."

"Aye." Rapsod stepped out, leaving Madelyn alone with the captain.

He watched her from across the table. Her tears continued to fall of their own accord. "I'm sorry," she said.

"Aye. Well. We'll figure something out. You'll get us home, one way or another." He turned away and returned to the deck.

Madelyn took a few steps back and collapsed onto the bed. She let the sobs come now. All the fear, all the sorrow, all of it in the song had sunk so deeply into her heart. She felt their pain and their horror at being in a place that didn't work the way they'd always known it to.

These were pirates, but they had left familiar waters. And they thought Madelyn could bring them home. Somehow. She wished that was true.

The ship turned ponderously. The wind picked up. Madelyn felt the ship begin to move. Still she lay on the bed. Eventually, her tears dried.

And then something knocked on a window.

She jumped in surprise. Her eyes shot to the windows at the front of the cabin. Renity's face hung on the other side of the glass.

Madelyn barely suppressed a yelp. She rushed to her feet and dashed to the window, searching for some way to open it. Her hand found a small lever. As she pulled it, a pane of glass leaned into the room. She yanked at it, prying it open even farther.

Renity moved to the open window. With some tugging and uncomfortable bending, Madelyn pulled her into the room. Renity's rapier clattered through the opening. The edges of her cloak crackled icily. "Your skin!" Madelyn said. "You're so cold!" She grabbed a blanket off the bed and swaddled Renity in it.

Her teeth chattered. "Thanks," she said. "I've been hanging there a while."

"How did you get there?"

"I jumped across. When the ships were leaving. Been there ever since. Climbing around, trying to find a way in. Saw you on the bed there. Now I rescued you." Renity grinned even though she still shivered. "See? I'm rescuing you."

Madelyn smiled back, brushing some of Renity's brown hair out of her face. "You sure did."

"So now we can do the important part."

"What's that?"

Renity's grin grew. "Rescue Rapsod from the pirates."

CHAPTER NINE

Madelyn blinked at Renity. "Rapsod's a pirate."

"So?"

Madelyn blinked again. "No. He's a pirate. He raided the Island. And he doesn't want to stay with you! He wants to go home. I heard him. He's got a girl in every port. That's what the captain said." She put a hand on top of her friend's. "He used his magic on you. I'm sorry, Renity."

"What do you know?" Her lips weren't as blue anymore. "Fine. As soon as I'm warmed up, I'll find him and prove it to you. He loves me. Did you see the way he danced with me?" She shook her head. "You're too young to know what it's like to be in love."

"I'm not that much younger than you." Madelyn wrinkled her nose.

"Maybe not. But you still look a lot younger. And you act like you're still fourteen."

Madelyn flinched.

"I'm sorry. But it's true." Renity frowned. She sighed. "I'm sorry. I know it's a sore spot. Everyone else growing up and you stuck back there."

Madelyn stood and walked away. "Maybe I'm still young, all right? Maybe it's because I'm fae. I guess they age more slowly than humans. But you know what? I fought the pirates better than you did. You were tricked. And just because I'm younger than you, just because you took care of me for a while, doesn't mean I'm stupid." Her words started coming faster and louder as she got worked up. "I'm the one who raised the Island. I'm the one who went out and rescued people."

"And I stayed on the Island and made sure everyone had enough to eat!" snapped Renity. "I'm the one who cleans up your messes, even when your mess is rescuing people!"

Madelyn felt the tears welling up behind her eyes. This was her friend. Her sister. The one who'd adopted her, taken care of her.

She closed her eyes and tried to get ahold of herself. She and Renity fought all the time, but she knew not to hit those sore spots. Like her age. Like how she wasn't responsible for everything. Renity loved her.

But this wasn't really her, was it? Rapsod had tricked her.

And if Rapsod had tricked Renity, did that mean maybe he'd tricked her too?

Were the pirates really just trying to get home? They wanted to get to the Bridge, yes. And they thought they needed her to do it. But they had attacked the Island, hadn't they? What good was the word of a pirate?

She couldn't trust any of them. She couldn't even trust herself now, could she? She had been crying for pirates.

Madelyn turned back to Renity. She walked over and knelt near the bundle of blankets. "Renity. They've messed us up. We just need to get away. For now, at least. If Rapsod really loves you, he'll find a way to come back to you, all right?"

Renity's face hardened.

Madelyn swallowed. Renity thought she was young? Thought she was helpless? All right. Then she'd be helpless, if it meant Renity would leave with her. "I need you to rescue me first. Then maybe we can come back and rescue Rapsod, all right? He's lived this long with the pirates. He can handle a little bit more." Madelyn paused and swallowed her bravado as best she could. "Rescue me," she pleaded. Oh, those words tasted so wrong.

She could see the thoughts racing through Renity's mind. She watched the various expressions chase each other across her face. Mercy. Love. Disgust. Indecision.

Madelyn took her hands. "I need you to come with me. To make sure I get home."

Renity breathed. She just breathed. And then she nodded, just a tiny, tiny little nod. "All right. You need rescuing. Fine. But I'm coming back for Rapsod once you're safe, all right? You're not the only one who can rescue people."

"Of course." Madelyn almost laughed in relief. "Of course. But we need to figure out some way to get off the skyships. Without, you know, falling to our deaths."

"Yeah. I suppose dying would be a bad way to end a rescue." Renity smiled back. She almost sounded like herself again. "Any ideas?"

Madelyn leaned back, sitting on the wood plank floor. "Not really. But I didn't really have the chance to think about it before." She was quiet for a moment, lost in thought. "Well, I can't fly.

And neither can you. And using a sword probably wouldn't help us against a whole crew of pirates."

Her friend nodded. "But you can float rocks."

"But I can float rocks."

"And floating rocks are what keep this ship up."

"Yeah. So?"

"So . . . We get one of the rocks free? And just float away?"

Madelyn grinned. "I like your plan."

Renity glanced back to the window she'd climbed through. "We could probably climb up the lines to the rocks through there. Well, I can. You climb like a fish."

"Hey! Just because you're part squirrel doesn't mean I can't climb!" Madelyn was starting to feel more like herself, too. Her gloom and fear started to dissipate. Sure, she was trapped on a pirate ship far from home, but they hadn't bothered to take her cutlass from her. Why would they? She was no threat.

Or so they thought.

She was Madelyn of the Sky. She'd failed to protect her Island, but she'd make it home. She'd rescue Renity. And once Grandma got back from Valan, there would be someone smart enough to keep these fae pirates away for good.

Madelyn hopped up and drew her cutlass. She spun it with a flourish. "Well, come on, Renity. It's time to free a stone from pirate subjugation. You know the way."

Renity nodded and stood, letting the blanket pool on the ground around her. "It's cold out there. You sure you'll be all right?"

Madelyn glanced around the cabin. Grinning, she grabbed a cloak that hung from a peg. She drew the cloak around herself. It wasn't the one Grandma had made for her, full of pockets, but it would do. "I'll be fine. Start climbing, if your big butt can fit out the window!"

Renity stuck her tongue out and turned back to the still-open window. Soon enough, she'd wriggled out. Madelyn sheathed her cutlass and followed.

It really was cold out here. The wind bit cold, even through the cloak. Night had fallen. The moon was a sliver in the sky, not letting out much light. The skyships must have been descending, though. Clouds were starting to reach up toward them. The feather in her hat fluttered in the wind.

The boat itself was covered in intricate carvings. Madelyn hadn't appreciated the craftsmanship when they had first approached the Island, mistaking the shapes as shabbiness. This close, she spotted wood whittled into the shapes of people and trees and storms and stones and other things she couldn't identify. Some sort of flying creatures? Fire in the shape of a fish?

Well, whatever the carvings were, it made clinging to the exterior of the ship relatively simple. They provided plenty of handholds and footholds. No wonder Renity had been able to climb so easily. Madelyn's friend began hauling herself upward with a whisper. "Most of the crew seem to be paying more attention to the sails on either side. We can head straight up here, I think."

Madelyn followed. The clouds began to swirl at her feet as the boat sunk lower in the sky. The mists coated the carvings in a wet sheen. She could still hang on, but it took more strength than before. She hoped it wouldn't take much skill to make it up the lines to the stones.

Renity climbed up to a small ledge and waited. Madelyn caught up.

"This is the railing. Once we climb above this, the pirates will be able to see us. See that line there? That's one of the ones anchoring the ship to the tarp. At least, it's a line leading up that way. We sidle up that, and then it's your show."

Madelyn nodded. "So we need to be fast."

"You need to be fast. I just need to move at my normal speed," Renity answered.

Oh, it felt good to be snide at each other again. Much better than whatever Renity had been doing when she thought she was in love with Rapsod.

By now, they'd descended fully into the cloud. It hung damp around them. Somewhere in the distance, something rumbled.

"A dragon?" Renity asked.

Madelyn shook her head. "Thunder, I think."

"They're flying into a thunderstorm?"

She shrugged. "Just one more reason to get out of here, right?"

Renity nodded and poked her head above the rail. She ducked again. "We'll have to wait just a minute. There's a lot of people up on the deck right now."

"What're they doing?"

"Boat things. I don't know! I was never in any navy!"

They clung to the hull. The mist soaked through Madelyn's cloak. She wrinkled her nose.

"What's wrong?" Renity asked in a whisper.

"I hate being cold."

"I warned you!"

84

"Yeah, well, that still doesn't mean I have to like it."

She shook her head. "Next time I'll make sure the pirates keep everything nice and warm for you."

And that's when it began to rain. Drops pelted them with icy water.

"Is that better?" Renity asked.

"Would you start climbing?" Madelyn said, gesturing to the line.

Renity poked her head over the rail again and then ducked. "Looks as good as any time," she said. "See you up top!"

"I'll see your big butt while you're climbing ahead of me."

"Well, at least it's my good side," Renity said as she reached for the line. She tugged it once. When she knew it was secure, she hauled herself upward as fast as she could.

Madelyn waited just a few moments, letting her friend get ahead of her. She listened for the cry of a pirate spotting her. None came.

She took a deep breath and reached for the line. She tugged it. Still secure as far as she could tell. The rain really was pelting her now. Hopefully it lowered visibility so there was less chance of the pirates catching them.

She stood, stepped onto the rail, and jumped as high as she could to give herself a good start on climbing. Hand over hand, she pulled herself up. The tight cords bit into her hands. She clamped her feet below. She couldn't wrap the rope around a foot to lock it. The line was just too tight. She'd have to depend on her own strength to keep her going.

Hand over hand. Hand over hand. Just keep going.

Her right hand slipped. She clenched every muscle to keep from falling. Her heart thundered louder than the wind. The rain dripped into her eyes. It was hard to see, but at least there still weren't any cries from the pirates.

She took a deep breath to steady her nerves and raised her hand to pull herself up again. The line was so slick.

And then her feet lost their grip. They fell off the line. She hung by just her fingers. Her legs swung wildly. Her weight was too much. The soaked cloak pulled at her neck and shoulders. Her boots felt far too heavy. Her fingers slid off the line.

She fell to the deck in a pile of girl, clothing, and cutlass.

As fast as she could, she jumped to her feet. She drew her blade.

Yep. The pirates had noticed that. A group of them turned toward the sudden noise. "Captain!" one called.

Carangth must not have been far away. He clomped into view and narrowed his eyes.

Madelyn tilted her head, letting her bravado out. "Well, Captain, I just wanted another chance to duel you. Shall we?"

Chapter Ten

"M iss, you were meant to stay in my cabin." Captain Carangth looked hurt. "It's not good for you to be wandering the ship when you don't know the rhythm of our life. You could end up hurt, and that would grieve us all."

Madelyn allowed herself to smile. Yes, this captain had bested her before. He knew how to duel like few did. But when she was backed into a corner, that's when she puffed up her chest and stood her ground. "It would take more than just you to cause anyone grief, Captain. If any of these gentlemen would like to try their hand against me, well, I suppose calling them gentlemen is a bit generous, isn't it?" She saluted the pirates who were gathering around.

Rapsod stood on the other side of the deck. Guri wasn't far away. Even the fae who had grown vines around Madelyn's ankles was there.

That pretty much meant there was no chance for her to win in a fight. Not if she played fair. What was it the captain had said? They wanted to go home? That human lands worked strangely? She hoped Renity was listening.

"You should know, you've taken me from my home. And the land doesn't like that so much." She lifted her chin and hollered as loud as she could. The rain was coming down hard, though they were sheltered from the worst of it here under the canopy of stones. "Fae aren't the only ones with power. You know that humans have their own charms, don't you? If you don't release me, I'll make sure this ship never flies again!"

The fae waited. They watched. The deck creaked. Rain beat against the side of the vessel.

"I said, I'll make sure this ship never flies again!" she cried out again.

This time something happened. The line nearest to Madelyn went slack. The entire ship tipped as it lost one of its connections to the floating stones. Lightning flashed. Pirates cried out in fear. Madelyn nearly lost her footing.

The captain didn't move his eyes from her. "Gjemb," he said, voice cutting through the noise, "vines. Now."

"Aye," one of the pirates said. She whispered to the deck. The wooden planking sprouted. Vines shot up and wrapped around the tarp, binding the ship to the stones again.

"Well, that's a new one." Madelyn grinned. "You better hope I don't call down any more problems! Stay here, or I'll make sure you lose all the lines!" She sheathed her blade, turned, and scampered up the vines as quickly as she could. These were hardly the smooth, straight line. She made it to the top of the tarp before any pirates could react.

Rain lashed at her as she clambered on top of the tarp. Renity grabbed her hand and helped her to her feet. "Nice plan," she shouted.

Lightning flashed through the clouds. Both girls flinched at the immediate boom.

Madelyn drew her cutlass. "Keep hacking!" She dashed to the next line and began sawing at it.

And then someone stood before her. Captain Carangth scowled through his beard. "Miss, that's enough. And you, too, stowaway." He nodded toward Renity. "I don't know how you managed to

90

get her on my ship, but this nonsense ends here." He drew his rapier.

"I already broke one of your rapiers. You think I can't do it to another?" Madelyn took a few steps back to put some distance between the two of them. Her feet slid as she took her stance. Water puddled here and there. "I suppose you can always beat me if you cheat," she spat.

"I'll do what I need to get my people home. I thought you understood that. I thought you agreed." He loomed a few steps closer. "I didn't expect you to go back on your word."

Madelyn felt a pang in her heart. She shoved it down. "You tricked me. You used Rapsod to enchant me." She retreated again, keeping her distance. Her feet slid, but she kept her footing. As long as she kept away from the edge, she should be safe. At least, that's what she told herself.

The entire canopy surged. Madelyn fell to her side, banging her elbow. Her grasp loosened on her cutlass for just a moment. Thankfully, she didn't lose it. She drove her fingers into the tarp, trying to find something to hold onto. Her body slid a foot, two, toward the edge. The captain cried a curse and fell, sliding sideways. The edge loomed.

There wasn't anything to catch them if they slipped over the edge. Nothing to protect them from an impossible drop.

An idea snapped through Madelyn's mind. She called the sparks from her heart and into her fingertips. No time to slice through the tarp. She'd never done this before, but there wasn't any other choice. She spoke to the stone through the tarp.

It answered.

The rocks beneath the tarp lifted, creating a cradle which caught her. Nothing caught Captain Carangth. He reached up with his rapier and slammed it into the tarp. The dagger shot from his other sleeve. He slammed that into the tarp, too. The tips of the blades caught. They tore at the fabric. After another foot of falling, he came to a stop. His feet dangled off the edge.

Thunder boomed.

Renity laughed over the storm. "Like that? I'll cut more lines. Let's see you fight like that!"

Madelyn cheered. Renity could climb anything. She could handle a wet tarp and keep her feet!

"What was that about cheating?" the captain called. "Go ahead, miss. Call me a pirate. Call me names! But then do the same thing yourself. You protect your people. I protect mine. And if that means kidnapping you, well, I'll do it!" He roared a laugh as he hung by his blades.

"I'm going home. Don't come after me." Madelyn stood in her cradle of stone. Using her cutlass, she sliced through the tarp so she could get to the bare rock. She'd been able to speak to it through the interference before, but it was best not to push it. "Renity! Come on. We can take this rock home."

Renity slid down the surface toward her.

"Run! Run and hide!" Carangth roared. He scrambled up onto his feet. His boots slid just a few inches. Lightning lit his fearsome face. He glanced down over the edge and then back toward Madelyn.

Renity slid into the cradle. Madelyn spread her fingers to speak to the stone. Wouldn't you like to float free?

Before the stone could respond, the captain sprinted toward them. He hurtled into Madelyn, slamming against her with his body. The two fell out of the cradle and slid toward the edge.

Renity screamed.

Madelyn's cutlass flew out of her grasp. It spun into the darkness. Water streamed from the sky over her face. She slapped her hands against the tarp. The captain laughed. She felt the edge vanish before she summoned any sparks.

They fell.

Her stomach lurched. Nothing underneath her. Nothing but sky. Nothing but the earth far, far below, somewhere. For a few moments, there was only the sound of rushing wind. Only her heart thundering. Only falling with the rain. Somewhere nearby, the captain laughed as lightning split the sky.

Then suddenly, all the air whooshed out of her lungs. Something had caught her! She struggled against the—was that fabric? She forced herself to her knees. Finally, she saw. The sails, the wide sails to the side of the ship, had caught them. The captain laughed nearby, struggling to his knees as well.

She didn't have time to think. She lunged toward the huge man. They collided and fell in a tangle of arms and legs. Her hand wrapped around his rapier in the tussle. Then she flung her legs around and somersaulted over his form.

Madelyn knelt facing him a few feet away. Rain dripped off the brim of her hat. She plunged the tip of the rapier down through the sail. It tore. "Well, Captain, there anything else to catch us if we fall again? What happens if I tear a hole through the sail?"

The laughter vanished from the captain's face. "You've had a fair flight. But it's over now. No reason to do that."

Madelyn heaved for breath. "I want to go home. I'll take a stone. My friend and I will leave. Simple as that. Let me go, and you live."

"I let you go, and none of my crew ever gets home again."

"That's fine by me," she answered. She finally had the chance to glance around. They'd slid far from the boat. On the deck, the woman who had called vines worked. Tendrils grew and wrapped around the tarp. The entire boat shifted, raising the side she and the captain knelt on. It tipped, raising Madelyn higher and higher into the sky. Water streamed off her. It fell from the sail in sheets. Thunder rolled in the distance.

The captain shook his head. "No, miss. You need to come with us."

She glanced behind her. A wooden cross brace lay there. She reached for it and held on tight. "You're not taking me anywhere." She raised the rapier to strike at the sail. The metal gleamed in the rain.

Lightning struck.

White fire shocked through the rapier, through Madelyn, down through the hull of the boat and down to the ground below. All that power flowed through her, burning her, lighting her up. She could not hear her scream over the sound of her pain.

But somehow she knew. Everyone on the ship did. Everyone on the other ships did. Everyone turned to the south. They saw the brilliant green flash.

"Home," the captain whispered.

Madelyn collapsed. The captain caught her. "There, miss," he said. "I've got you. You won't fall. And you'll see us home yet."

Chapter Eleven

Madelyn woke on her cot back at the Island. Pale light shone through the windows. It smelled like fresh bread, the kind Grandma always used to bring back from the market, back when they'd still lived on the ground.

Grandma waited nearby, her hands on her hips. "About time you went to sleep. Now, where are they taking you?"

Madelyn groaned as she sat up and rubbed her eyes. "To the Bridge. If they can find it."

"What do you mean, 'if they can find it'?" Grandma snapped. "They must have crossed over. It's not like you can just stumble across."

Madelyn took a deep breath. "So. You're talking to me in my dreams. I guess that means I'm not dead, right?"

"I've never been able to talk to dead people, no."

"Well, that's good. I was struck by lightning. I think. We were in a thunderstorm, and I had a rapier." She shook her head. "Everything burned, and then I woke up here. Well, you found me dreaming, I guess."

Grandma sat next to her and placed a hand against Madelyn's forehead. She murmured to herself for a moment before addressing her granddaughter, "I think you'll be fine. You've been hurt. Badly. But someone's taking care of you, near as I can tell."

"They want me healthy. They think I can guide them back to Fae."

"Why would they think that?"

Madelyn gestured around her dream of her home. "Because I don't belong here and I don't belong there. Their captain said I was like a compass, so maybe I could guide them to the Bridge."

"It still doesn't make any sense. You can't cross over by accident."

"Peter did."

"Well, that friend of yours is an idiot, isn't he?"

Usually, Madelyn would giggle at that, but she wasn't exactly in the mood. "How long do we get to dream-talk?"

"Until you wake up. I went to sleep myself the moment Essica's pigeons found me."

"Which ones?"

"The ones that said the Island was pillaged by air pirates and that they were looking for you." Grandma held up a hand. "Before you ask, Essica said no one was seriously hurt. A lot of people are scared, especially with you gone, but they're all fine now. Even Essica. Miah had to chip away at the stone that wrapped around her for a while, though."

"Peter too?"

Grandma scowled at her question. "Yes. Him too."

Madelyn felt herself relax. "Good. Yes." She nodded.

"We need to get you back before the Island falls."

"When will you get back to the Island?" she asked.

"Not until I get you back!"

"There's a woman here. A girl. She looks younger than me, but she says she's thirty. She can speak to stone better than I can. She said she convinced the Island to stay in the sky. That I wouldn't need to be there anymore."

Grandma crossed her arms and regarded her granddaughter. "Really? You believe her?"

"Why wouldn't I?"

"She's a pirate, isn't she? She wanted you to come along peacefully. I'm betting you didn't fight nearly as hard once you knew the Island was taken care of."

Madelyn shook her head. "I thought fae couldn't lie."

"We can't. But that doesn't mean we always tell the truth." She sighed. "So. The Bridge. I'll be able to meet you there. I'll gather up Aralane and his best men. Maybe get some archers if I can track any down. And then we'll force the pirates to give you back."

Madelyn stared at a spot on the wall. "What if Guri was right though? What if the Island doesn't need me?"

"What are you blathering about?"

She looked down. "If the Island doesn't need me, you shouldn't get all those people to come find me. I'm not that important. Too many people could get hurt."

"Granddaughter, I carried you from Fae to keep you safe. I would go to war for you, sacrifice anything for you. You're growing. You can do so much on your own. I understand that. But now? When you've been captured? I will follow you back into Fae, into the dark, into the endless winter where sun will never warm stone again to rescue you."

Madelyn shook her head. "I'm not worth that."

Grandma burst into laughter. Madelyn jumped at the unexpected sound. "Not worth it? Granddaughter, you don't get to decide that. No one decides their own worth. I've found that when people try, they always get it wrong. Always." She brushed a strand of hair from Madelyn's face. "Some people think far too much of themselves. And others? Far too little. You, Granddaughter, have rescued so many. Now it is our turn to rescue you."

Madelyn stood and paced to the other side of the room. "But you don't need me. Don't put yourself at risk. Not anyone else either. Besides, I can save myself. I'll figure a way out of here."

Grandma barked a laugh. "I will rescue you because I love you. And that is enough." She rose and followed Madelyn across the room. "Your value does not lie in what you do. If it did, you would never know if you had value. Now. I know where you're going. I'll meet you there with enough people to rescue you. Just stay alive until then."

She frowned. "I don't like this." She was the rescuer. The Island didn't need her to keep floating anymore, but she could still rescue people. That's who she was. But now, if she needed rescuing again? Everything was upside down.

"You don't have to like it. Most days you don't like me very much anyway."

"Only because you whack me upside the head!"

"I only do that when you're being an idiot." Grandma chuckled. "I should probably be doing that right now." She sobered. "Now. What else do I need to know? Tell me everything you can."

And Madelyn did, from the first moment Renity spotted the pirates until the lightning strike. Grandma listened carefully, nodding along and asking questions to make sure she understood everything well.

"Do you know about these pirates, Grandma?" Madelyn asked when she reached the end of her story.

Grandma shook her head. "Every House has criminals. In Fae many punishments are meted out. Sometimes death. Sometimes imprisonment. And sometimes exile. Those in exile sometimes band together. My guess is that you've found such a group."

"Do you think they really just want to go home?"

"Oh, they want to go home. The human realm is vast and terrifying. It doesn't work by our rules. And the people here are truly intoxicating."

"What do you mean?"

Grandma chuckled now. "Humans say fae are fickle and seductive. And we are, in our way. But truly, we simply live by different rules. And things that are different might entice someone tired of their own life. And humans? They're different from us. For a fae who is disenchanted with their life, say, an exile, the human world is very attractive."

"Is that why you brought us here?"

"No. I brought us here to escape the disaster."

"But if there's a disaster in Fae, why would they go back?"

"Granddaughter, a disaster can move so slowly many don't recognize it. So for now, it seems these pirates of yours don't know what's happening in their own home."

The light outside the room brightened.

"It looks like you'll be waking soon," Grandma said.

Madelyn felt so torn. She wanted rescue. She didn't want to risk anyone else. She wanted to rescue herself. She could do something, right?

It was impossible.

She couldn't find words.

"Hush, Granddaughter. You fought well to protect your people. Now let your people fight for you." Grandma smiled and spread her arms.

Madelyn embraced her until the light swallowed her and she woke from the dream.

CHAPTER TWELVE

M adelyn woke lying on the huge bed in the captain's quarters. Every joint in her body, from her toes to her neck, ached. She was so, so thirsty.

As she stirred, a form rose over her. "Here." Someone placed a glass against her lips. She drank sweet, cool water. The glass pulled away before she had taken more than three swallows. "Not so much. A little at a time, or you'll get sick. And I don't think anyone wants to clean up after you."

Madelyn pried her eyes open to see Captain Carangth sitting next to the bed, holding the glass of water.

"How'd you get the water so cold?" Madelyn asked.

The captain chuckled. "House Frostburn doesn't like using its powers for convenience, but those who have been exiled don't mind so much." He raised the glass for her again. "Plus it's freezing out there. Here. Just a few more swallows."

Madelyn took a little more water.

"Not many would survive a lightning blast, miss. And fewer still are those who know how to treat such injuries. You're lucky on two counts." He placed the glass on a nearby table, next to a pitcher that dripped with condensation. "And now we're pointed toward the Bridge. Toward home."

"You look sad."

"Aye."

"Why would you be sad?"

The captain sighed. "We never meant to be in your world. We were running and slipped over the border. Usually, we only raid ports that, well, you don't need to know what things are like in Fae. We're not used to encountering anyone who hasn't taken sides. But, miss, you should know that you put up a good fight. More than one good fight, in fact."

"You're not answering the question."

"You're very forceful for a young lady who's not strong enough to get herself a drink of water."

"You could have killed me if you wanted. Instead, you kept me safe. Carried me in from the sail.

Cared for me for I don't know how long. I figure I can push a little."

The captain barked a laugh. "Well, then. I'm sad because you have fire in you. And you're not someone fighting us. Not really. But, well . . ." He looked away. "Did you see the flash in the distance?"

"I think so. Something green?"

"Aye. Every member of my crew felt its pull. It was the Bridge, lighting our way, calling us home. We were able to take a heading. The entire fleet's going home." He looked away.

"That's good, though," Madelyn said. "Everyone's excited to go home, right?" Why did Carangth look so upset? He had what he wanted now. They were going back to Fae.

"Aye. It's good. But it's not enough. All we got was a heading. We don't know where we're going. How far."

Madelyn thought for a moment. "So what gave it that green flash? What made the Bridge light up?"

He looked at her.

"What?"

"You did, miss." He sighed as he stood. "When you were in pain, something in you called to the Bridge. I think it might be because you're not of this world and not of ours. So part of you belongs to that Bridge. And well, when you called out, the Bridge answered. It called to you."

Madelyn swallowed. "So what are you saying?"

"We take our heading from the Bridge. So the only way for us to find our way home is to make the Bridge call out to you again. And again. Until we find it." He looked away. "And the only way to do that is to cause you great pain."

Madelyn's heart thundered. "I need to be struck by lightning again?" Her voice shook. She already couldn't move. Everything in her hurt. She couldn't do that again. Not again. No. She'd face impossible odds without blinking, but that kind of pain?

"No. Not lightning. At least, we don't think so. But pain." He swallowed. He paced. "I could make you, you know. I could just give you to some of my crew, and they'd do whatever it took to get home. I could even make you want to. I could bring Rapsod in here. He'd sing you a song so sad you'd beg to be hurt again." He stopped pacing and finally looked at her.

Madelyn tried to find words, but none came. Here she was. She couldn't move. She couldn't do anything. And the captain knew it.

Carangth's jaw seemed to creak as he worked out the next words. "I can't do that to you. I can't hurt someone like that. It's not battle." He shook. "But my crew . . . I'm willing to be exiled here. I've already been exiled from my home. What's one more realm? But I can't do that to them. Oh, miss. I wish there was another way, but there's not. And I will not do that to you. Not to one so brave as yourself."

He only wanted to bring his people home. He wanted to protect his people.

But what if it was a trick? Madelyn knew what Grandma would say. Of course it was a trick. Peter would probably say the same thing.

Renity would want her to help, probably, if only to help Rapsod. But she was enchanted. That wasn't really Renity. Not that part of her, at least.

But she did need to get to the Bridge. Grandma would be waiting there. She couldn't get free unless she got to the Bridge. Even if the captain didn't want to hurt her, that didn't mean he was going to let her go free or return her to the Island.

But fae couldn't lie. He just said he wouldn't hurt her. He was telling the truth, wasn't he?

"What will you do with me?"

"I don't know," he answered. "If I let you go, the crew might mutiny. They know you're the key, especially now."

"What will you do with Renity?"

"Your friend? I don't think she'll ever leave. She keeps following Rapsod around like a little moth following a wisp."

"What if . . ." Madelyn closed her eyes. Did she want to do this?

No. She didn't want to do this.

But was it the right thing to do? Her fingers rubbed against each other, as if worrying the hem of her shirt. She couldn't move more than that, though. Not through her pain and weakness.

"What if I gave myself willingly? What if I let you hurt me? I bring you to the Bridge. And when we get there, you leave me and Renity behind. You go home. We go home."

The captain frowned. "I don't know how badly we'll have to hurt you."

"I know." She tried so hard to keep her voice steady.

"And your friend will hate you for taking her from Rapsod."

"We'll find a way to survive."

"Do you give your word? You won't run. You won't flee. You give yourself willingly until we reach the Bridge. And should you keep your word, I will see that you're hurt no more than necessary to guide us. You'll be free on any of the ships of the fleet. And when we reach the Bridge, you and your friend go free. Should you give your word, on oath, I give mine." He held out his hand.

Madelyn grunted with effort. Her shoulder screamed. Her elbow bellowed. Her wrist yelled. But at last, she freed her arm from the blankets and placed her hand in the captain's.

"Agreed."

CHAPTER THIRTEEN

R enity sat beside her on the bed. "You awake
this time?" she asked.

Madelyn took a deep breath. "I think? I don't
want to be."

"Well, that must mean you're almost normal."
Renity took a glass of water from a table beside the
bed and held it out to her friend. "They told me to
make sure you were drinking plenty of water."

Madelyn reached for the glass. As she did, her
elbow and knuckles burned. The pain was quiet,
but very present. That changed when she took the
weight of the glass. She cried out against the sudden hurt. The glass fell onto the blankets, splash-
ing water all over.

"Sorry," Renity said. She snatched the glass from
the blankets. "I'll get you some more water."

"What's wrong, Renity?"

"You're in pain." She stood with a sigh. "I should have realized you couldn't hold the glass."

"No. That's not what I'm talking about." She flexed her fingers, feeling the pain subside back to that gentle burn. "I dropped a glass of water. You should be making fun of me."

"It's not nice to tease someone who's already down."

Madelyn shook her head and immediately regretted it. "Normally. But you always make fun of me. It's how you show love."

Renity didn't answer for a moment. "I'm going to get you some more water." She padded out of the cabin, leaving her alone. Madelyn glanced at the table next to her. The pitcher still sat on it, dripping condensation.

She leaned back against the pillow. The cool water continued to soak through the blankets, but apparently not enough to get through the layers of fabric to where she lay. At least there was that. She didn't have the strength to change the bedding. What was wrong with Renity, though?

Well, she was on a pirate ship flying away from everything she ever knew.

But Renity loved adventure. She'd always climbed everywhere, trying to see what was beyond the next hill. This should just be another adventure. She even chose to come on this adventure, unlike Madelyn.

But she'd been enchanted by that fae, Rapsod, hadn't she?

Renity came back into the cabin. Her feet were quiet on the wood planks. Madelyn glanced down and noticed she was barefoot. "Where are your shoes?" she asked.

Renity glanced down at her feet. "What? Oh. All the sailors go barefoot, even the captain. It helps them balance and keep their feet better. I thought I'd do what everyone else was doing if it helped so much." She shrugged. "Here." She sat on the bed and held the glass to Madelyn's lips.

She drank a few swallows. "Thank you," she said.

"The captain said you made some sort of deal with him."

"Yeah." Madelyn leaned back against her pillow again. "We're going to get home."

"You think that's a good idea? Making a deal with a pirate captain? Didn't you say they were the bad guys or something?"

"I'm just trying to get us home."

"Good." She didn't smile when she said it.

"Renity? What's wrong?"

She sighed again. She shook her head.

"Come on. You can tell me anything. You know you can. You told me when you stole your mom's hairbrush. And when you and Martin kissed. We're sisters; we tell each other everything." Madelyn reached for her hand and took it.

Renity grimaced. "I thought you were going to die."

"You've thought that before. Like when I was chained up in Valan. You didn't act like this then. I was there. I remember."

"Maybe I don't want to talk about it, all right?"

Madelyn tried to be quiet. She did. Outside, men called to each other. A song started up. The ship tipped to the right just slightly. The lanterns that hung from the ceiling swayed.

What could make Renity like this? The two of them shared everything with each other. There were no secrets between them. From the first time Renity got in trouble through the first time Madelyn could float stone, they shared their lives. Only something that hurt Renity a lot would keep her mouth shut.

And then Madelyn knew. "Did something happen with Rapsod?"

Renity sat quietly for a while longer. "You were right. He was tricking me. He told me. And then he told me I had to leave him alone because I was casting a spell on him." She shook her head. "Me? Right." She pressed her lips together, her eyes on her lap.

The younger woman didn't know what to say. She finally stuttered out, "I'm sorry."

Renity didn't answer. Instead, she set the glass on the table and walked back to the door. On her way, she bumped into the table. Ripples spread across its surface as she opened the door. Renity didn't notice. By the time she'd shut the door behind her, a face appeared above the table.

Rapsod's face.

It stared at Madelyn a few moments before vanishing in more ripples.

CHAPTER FOURTEEN

H ow long?" Madelyn asked.

She stood at the very front of the skyship, letting the wind run through her hair. It felt clean in a way that was hard to describe, in a way that not even the wind on the Island felt. The Island's wind felt like home. The wind here felt like freedom, even though she was trapped.

The captain loomed behind her. "Soon," he answered. "The heading we took when you were struck by lighning was a good start. But we'll need to take one again soon."

"What are you going to do?"

The captain swallowed before answering. "We stole some things from House Tempest. Didn't want them using them on us. I didn't expect to be using them ourselves."

"What are they?"

The captain didn't answer for a moment. "Iron cutlasses."

"I was held in iron shackles before," Madelyn said. She shivered as she remembered the sound of her skin hissing against the cold metal.

"Well, we won't be stabbing you with them. But what I will do is hold the flat of the blade against your skin. You choose where. And I'll only do it until we can get a heading." He looked away. "I just hope it's fast."

"How many people have you killed, Captain?"

"Ah. Too many, from each of the thirteen Houses."

"You've killed, but you don't want to harm me."

He grunted a low laugh. "We're not battling, are we?"

"But I killed some of your crew, didn't I? I knocked some off the edge when you struck the Island."

"What was done there was done to defend you and yours. I don't count that against anyone." He shook his head. "But as I said, we're not battling now. Now you're aiding my crew. And I gave you my word. You'll not be hurt any more than is necessary."

Madelyn felt a guilty stirring in her gut. When she brought them to the Bridge, even with the pain it would cause her, there would be people waiting for them. She wasn't aiding them at all. She was bringing them in sight of their home, only to strike at them. The idea nibbled at her.

She shook her guilt off. Well, she tried to. "Do you know what we're flying over?" She looked down over the edge of the deck. The cloud cover had dissipated, revealing a rolling brown land with patches of brilliant green. The Island always hovered over silver fog, so this was a new sight for her. It was beautiful.

"South." The captain shrugged.

"Probably Ebhold, then. Most of the people on the Island are from here. They always said their land was beautiful." She nodded. "It is, isn't it?"

"Beauty and danger often go together." The captain glanced over his shoulder. "Come, miss."

"Why do you keep calling me that? You called Guri *lass.*"

"Women on the crew are *lass*. They've won the right to be called that. You? You're not crew here. You don't belong here. You're *miss*. And now, we need to take a new heading. Come." He held out his hand.

119

JONATHON MAST

Madelyn placed hers in the offered hand. He guided her to the center of the deck. Rapsod waited nearby. Renity stood across from him. "What are they going to do?" She aimed the question at Rapsod.

The tall fae's face remained carefully impassive. "What we have to."

She turned back toward Madelyn. "What are they doing, sis?"

"I'm keeping my end of the deal so we get to go home." Madelyn swallowed. Captain Carangth said they'd press the blades wherever she chose. But where was a good place to choose pain? She flinched as she remembered what happened when the iron shackles were placed on her.

Guri sat on the edge of the deck, her oversized cloak draping her form and flowing onto the deck. She sighed.

Others gathered. A stooped form brought forth a chest that seemed alive with leaves. A fae, the one who had grown the vines to the canopy of stones, stepped up to it. She breathed, and the chest bloomed. Inside lay seven dull-gray blades. As the midday light revealed them, every fae instinctively leaned away.

Madelyn found it was hard to breathe.

"Gjemb. Get our compass a chair," the captain instructed.

The woman turned and nodded. Soon the deck sprouted a simple stool. Madelyn sat on it and bent over, cradling her stomach.

Renity stepped close and took her hand. "Madelyn. What are they doing?"

A lanky fae with pale skin and bright green eyes stepped next to Madelyn. "Once the captain has the heading, I'll put you to sleep."

Madelyn looked up at her.

"I was cast out from House Slumber. Your sleep will be a mercy. It will swallow your pain."

And then Madelyn would be able to talk to her grandma again. She looked up at the lanky fae and nodded. "What's your name?"

"Dremit," she said.

"Thank you, Dremit."

The captain reached a hand into a pocket of his red, red coat and pulled out two thick leather gloves. "Miss. Have you chosen where you will feel the pain?"

Madelyn felt like she was going to throw up. "There's not a good place for pain."

He closed his eyes for a long moment before replying, "No. There's not."

She looked down at her body. Her hands? Her wrists? Her ankles? Her stomach? Not her face. She knew that much. She clenched her hands, holding back her nausea as best she could. "My wrists. Where the shackles were before. At least I know what the pain there is like."

"Aye." He nodded. "All hands! Eyes to the horizon! We want that heading as soon as possible!"

"Rapsod?" Renity murmured. "What are they doing? Madelyn? What are you doing?" She looked up at the fae she'd loved. "You danced with me. You owe me an explanation! Something!"

He flinched at her words. "Eyes to the horizon," he said.

The captain reached into the trunk and took hold of one of the blades. He cursed. His shoulder twitched. He lifted the sword, a wicked cutlass of iron. "Miss, hold out your hand."

Madelyn offered her right arm but then thought better of it. She lifted her left arm.

"Stuhi, adjust the wind the moment we have a heading. Don't waste a moment."

"Aye, Captain."

"Rapsod, control your woman."

"I'm not his woman."

"She's not my woman, Captain."

"She's your responsibility until we drop her off," he growled.

Rapsod moved beside Renity. She snarled at him. He backed away a step and said, "It must happen."

"What must happen? What's going on?" Now she was frantic. Her eyes shot between the captain and Madelyn. "Get away from her! Let me go. Get away from her!"

The captain held the blade in front of Madelyn. "I was hoping fear would be enough to make the Bridge call out to you. I'm sorry."

"Do it," Madelyn said. Her voice shook. She really was going to throw up if they didn't hurry.

"Dremit, are you ready?"

"Aye, Captain. The moment we have a heading."

Carangth nodded once. The blade spun in his hand. He pressed the flat of the sword against Madelyn's left wrist before she had the chance to gasp.

She heard the sizzle before she felt the pain. And then the hurt exploded from blackening skin. She probably screamed. She'd screamed last time. She couldn't hear anything over the pain. She didn't hear Renity screaming, cursing, threatening. She didn't hear Carangth calling out for a heading. She didn't hear the crew scrambling around the ship, watching, waiting. All she heard was her pain.

Then something flashed inside her eyelids. Someone called out. The captain removed the blade.

Dremit whispered something, and sleep took her.

Chapter Fifteen

R apsod says you're not under his control. He's pretty sure, anyway." Guri sat next to the captain's bed. Well, Madelyn's bed now. Carangth told her he'd taken a berth with the rest of the crew until they reached the Bridge.

Madelyn lay under a heavy quilt. Her wrist was wrapped, but she still felt queasy. "Well, that's good," she answered.

"He's not sure. It's not like he's ever sung for humans before. Usually, his spells end pretty quickly, but it lasted a long time for your friend. Until he told her she only loved him because of the spell."

"I thought that's what happened with them." Madelyn shook her head. "Maybe it's for the better, though. Now she won't fight when it's time to go home."

The other woman frowned. "Why are you helping us?"

"It's the right thing to do." Madelyn saw the confusion on Guri's face. "I help people find homes. You don't belong here. And, honestly, I don't want you staying on the Island. So the only choice is to get you back to Fae."

"But you're hurting. And I can tell you still have iron poisoning."

"Iron poisoning?"

"Iron hurts anyone with fae blood. Anyone. And it's not just the pain. It's like you're severed from your House for a while. The stones won't talk to you. We call it iron poisoning."

"Ah." Madelyn lifted her arm to look at the wrappings around her wrist. "I didn't know it had a name."

"It doesn't make any sense." Guri kept frowning. "Leaders don't give. It's the ones below who give. You're a leader. You protect your Island because it's yours. But you're nothing like any leader I've seen before. Except maybe the captain."

"What are leaders like in Fae?"

Guri looked out the window. The ship creaked as the wind pushed it along the new heading. The lamps shone their different colors. Finally,

Guri looked back. "They do what's best for their Houses. But what's best for the House isn't always what's best for the members of the House. Or even their own families."

"What do you mean?"

Guri shook her head. "I was House Stone. Like you. Our House sets its roots deeper than any other House. House Thorn cannot be removed long from the sun. Even House Eclipse cannot fathom the darkness we can revel in. We go so deep. Our House has many princes and princesses. But when we lose territory, a prince or princess must be sacrificed. There's not enough to support so many otherwise." She looked down at her hands.

"You were a princess?"

"I was. I fled."

"What would have happened if you stayed?"

Guri shook her head again. "Best not to dwell on that. Too many princes, too many princesses breeds battle within the House. And a House that fights itself? It doesn't last long."

Madelyn was silent for a long while. "So would you be my princess if I was there?"

Guri huffed a laugh. "I don't think so. I fled before you were born, young one."

"Hey! I'm twenty in human years!"

"Oh, I know. That's why you look so much older than I do." Guri shook her head. "But I fled long before that."

"House Stone would have killed you when you were that young?"

"Of course. It's far easier to kill a child than an adult who can defend herself." She shrugged. "But that's the way it is in Fae. The Houses are everything. And that's why I don't understand you. You're not protecting your House, your Island. You're helping someone who invaded. There's a goodness about that which I don't understand."

"Well, maybe I'm not as good as you think," Madelyn murmured.

Grandma hadn't been there in her sleep this last time. She must have been dealing with Prince Aralane or traveling to the Bridge already.

And what would happen then?

Did Madelyn want the pirates to get home? She didn't know. Guri didn't seem so bad. And the captain . . . Was he that bad? Were any of them? They just wanted to get home.

And she knew she didn't want anyone to fight for her. She didn't want Grandma to risk herself. She didn't want to have to be rescued by Prince Aralane, or anyone from Kenevir. That was for sure. But if Grandma made it to the Bridge before them, there would be a fight. And someone would get hurt.

And Madelyn knew she wasn't worth that.

She'd found a way to free herself and Renity. All it took was her pain. And she didn't want the pain, but if it meant freedom, if it meant getting the pirates to go home, well, that was fine. She'd deal with it.

She just hated all of it. She hated that she might be leading the pirates back to an awful place, if what Guri said about Fae was true. She hated that she might be getting her grandma and others involved in a fight. That she might be luring the pirates into battle. She felt dirty.

"Maybe you're far better than you think," Guri said.

Madelyn sighed.

"If we have the chance, after your iron poisoning wears off and before the next time we—" she faltered. "Before the next time we have to take a heading, I'll teach you how to do more things with stone. If you're going to give us your pain, the least I can do is give you my teaching."

Madelyn nodded. "All right. I can do that."

Guri stood. "You need to rest."

"I feel like I've been resting most of the time since you took me from the Island."

"That was a polite way of saying I'm going to go do something else now." Guri shook her head. "So don't rest if you don't want to. But I should go see to my duties." She turned and left the cabin.

As Guri stepped out, another woman stepped in. This was the woman who could grow plants from the deck, who had made a trunk blossom. Gjemb, the captain had called her.

"Madelyn of the Sky," she said, "you return us to our home fields. The crews have seen your courage for us."

"Don't tell me I'm a good person," Madelyn moaned.

"You force us to pay you."

"What?"

"This is the way with fae. No gift may be given unless another is returned. And now the crews of Captain Carangth are in your debt. Every single one of us."

"Why?"

"A flower cannot blossom unless the sun gives it light. And the flower repays the sun by blossoming. This is the way of the fae."

Madelyn looked at the door Guri had exited through. "Is that why Guri wants to teach me how to speak to stone better?"

"That is how her flower will blossom for you, yes."

It was just a payment. Guri wasn't trying to be a friend.

"Well," Madelyn said, "I guess you all owe me, then."

"A flower that will not blossom to the light poisons itself. Tell me how to blossom for you, Madelyn of the Sky."

"If you get home and leave us be, that'll be payment enough." Madelyn tried to roll away from Gjemb. This wasn't a conversation she wanted to have. She leaned on her wrist without thinking, though, and cried out in pain.

Gjemb stepped close. "I can grow berries that will relieve your pain." She reached a hand over the deck and whispered something.

Before any vines could sprout, Madelyn said, "No. I'm fine. I was just surprised. Stop it!"

Gjemb fell silent.

"You're leaving me behind when you get to the Bridge. That was the deal I made with Captain Carangth. Isn't that enough?"

131

"That is the deal you made with him, not with us."

"So I'll make that deal with you."

Gjemb shook her head. "We cannot enter into an agreement already made."

Madelyn felt suddenly tired. "All right. Let me think, all right? I didn't know you had to do something for me. Fine."

Gjemb nodded. "Do not wait long, Madelyn of the Sky." She turned and exited the captain's quarters.

CHAPTER SIXTEEN

Madelyn lay back against the pillow. The bed really was comfortable, better than her cot back at the Island. At least her pain was muted now. Her thoughts flitted back and forth.

Was she doing the right thing? The best thing?

She thought about Guri. A princess forced to flee when she was that young?

If the pirates were all exiles, did they all have stories like Guri's? If they did, were they the bad guys at all? Maybe it was good they were raiding the Houses if all the Houses were like hers.

Was everyone all right back at the Island? Had Peter woken up yet? Grandma had said he was fine . . . If Peter were here, what would he do? He'd probably have some snarky comment. He wouldn't want to help the pirates. But he would've just decayed the ropes holding the stones in place, and he and Madelyn would have soared into the sky free. And then Madelyn wouldn't have to ask these questions.

But now the pirates owed her. All of them. What was she supposed to do with that?

Should she try to escape again? No. She'd given her word. She'd get them to the Bridge. They should go home.

But was their home really any good?

Madelyn rolled over. She wished she knew more about fae, about their Houses, about these people who'd raided the Island and taken her. Maybe then she'd know whether to fight them or help them.

If only she knew them better.

She blinked. And then she smiled.

Renity banged into the room. Madelyn jumped and then groaned. Renity stomped over to her and crossed her arms. She glared.

"What'd I do?" asked Madelyn.

"Nothing. I'm not mad at you."

She blinked. "So what happened?"

"Rapsod's supposed to look after me. I'm his responsibility. As if I can't help out here by myself. As if I need a babysitter. As if I need *him* to be watching me. Carangth could have had anyone else watch out for me, but Rapsod? This is the first time I've been alone since you—" She stopped and glared at Madelyn directly. "Since you decided that you being hurt was the best way to help everyone."

Madelyn didn't know what to say. She lay in the bed, staring up at her friend.

"You shouldn't have done that," Renity said.

"What was I supposed to do? The pirates need to go home. And we need to go home. And that's the best way to do it."

"Who cares about the pirates? You shouldn't be hurt like that. I can't just watch them do that to you. Besides, they're pirates. Who cares if they get home? They're useless, and they dance with you, and they leave like that dance was nothing." Renity knelt by the bed and took Madelyn's hand in her own. "Trust me." Her voice shook. "They're not worth you hurting like that."

Madelyn searched her friend's face. "Fine. But you are. And I want to get you home."

Renity gave a sad chuckle. "I'm not worth that either. You're so much more important than I am. I don't do anything at the Island. You keep it flying. You rescue people. You're the important one here."

"No. No, I'm not." Madelyn struggled to sit up through the mound of blankets. "You're my friend. My sister. You took care of me when I was alone. And now I get to take care of you." She finally flung the last blanket off and seized Renity's hand. "You're worth it."

Renity glared. "No. I'm not. And I don't need to be saved. I don't need you or anyone else taking care of me." She yanked her hand away and surged to her feet.

Madelyn rose unsteadily. "I'm sorry. It's the only way I could figure out how to get them home. And us home."

Renity paced the cabin. "Next time, don't save me," she blurted.

"What?" Madelyn almost fell back onto the bed. "Don't save you? Renity, you came after me. And if you weren't there . . ." She felt a lump in her throat. "If you weren't there, I don't know what I'd do. You're my big sister. You took care of me." She made her way toward Renity. "I don't know what I'd do if I lost you."

"You'd be fine."

"No." She stopped a few feet away. "No, I wouldn't. I could fight the legions of Kenevir. I could fight all the pirates in the sky. But if I lost you, I wouldn't have my big sister anymore. I'll do anything to keep you safe. Anything. You're worth it."

Renity huffed.

Madelyn was close enough to see the tears running down Renity's face. "Ren, what's wrong? Please. Tell me."

"Nothing."

"Liar."

Renity glared again. "Rapsod used me. He made me fall in love with him. And then he turned off the dance. And now he says I'm 'intoxicating him' with my beauty. But he used me." She hugged herself. "And the thing is, I keep thinking about us dancing. About us fighting and how much fun it was. I was fighting for the Island, but I was laughing. And he was laughing. And . . . I want to dance like that again."

Now Madelyn's tears joined Renity's. "I'm so sorry. I'm sorry I couldn't save you from him."

"I don't want you to save me!" she snapped. "I just—I just need someone to listen. To tell me it'll be all right." She sighed. "I don't need you to fix it. I need you to be there."

Madelyn nodded. "I'm sorry." She reached out and took Renity's hands in her own. "I'm sorry. I'll listen."

Renity stepped closer. Her arms wrapped around Madelyn. She returned the embrace.

Madelyn's friend sobbed into her shoulder for a long time.

That evening, Captain Carangth entered the room. "Miss. Four bells. Supper." He stood aside, gesturing in some of his crew. They carried in a covered platter and some plates and set them on the expansive table.

Madelyn rose from the bench near the huge windows.

As the crew retreated, the captain tapped the table. Two chairs formed from the ripples.

"How does the table work?" Madelyn asked.

"Ah, it's a glamour, and a bit more. It shows you whatever you most want at that moment."

"You wanted chairs?"

"How else will we eat together?" Carangth grinned at her. "It does take practice to make sure it gives you a certain thing and not whatever else might flit through your mind. The first time I tapped the table, it showed me sausages. Made my mouth water for days, every time I thought of them."

Madelyn seated herself. "What's for supper?"

"Not much. Your Island didn't have much in the way of supplies. We were running low when we crossed over to human lands. And so many human foods are dangerous."

Madelyn laughed. "Really?"

The captain raised an eyebrow. "How do you know what's safe to eat and what isn't?"

"Potatoes are fine to eat. Apples. Most food!"

"And how do you know what part of a plant is food and what part isn't? How do you know what's safe to hunt and what will hunt you back? This is a foreign land, miss."

"And you just want to go home."

"Aye." The captain removed the cover from one of the platters, revealing sliced tomatoes sprinkled with herbs of some kind. "We think this is safe. No one's died from it yet."

"As far as I know, those are good." She took a slice and placed it on an empty plate. Tomatoes were hardly her favorite, but food was food. She took a bite, swallowing as quickly as possible to banish the taste.

"How are you feeling?"

"My wrist hurts, especially when I put any weight on it. The rest of me is fine, though. Just sore from the lightning bolt yet."

"Good." The captain served himself a slice of tomato and eyed it warily. "You're sure this is safe?"

Madelyn took another bite in answer. She really was hungry.

"Well." He nibbled at it and wrinkled his nose. "I look forward to returning to Fae. Food there doesn't taste like dirt."

She tried not to giggle.

"I'm sorry. Soon enough we'll need to take another heading. I suspect before your wrist heals."

Madelyn sobered quickly. Her stomach knotted. "How soon?"

"Too soon."

"Tonight?"

"Yes."

Madelyn swallowed and put her fork down. "Your crew owes me."

"They're in your debt, yes. And not happy about it."

"Gjemb told me. I've been thinking about how they might pay that debt."

The captain raised his eyebrows. "How?"

"I want to hear their stories. Why they're here, in your skyship. And I want to start with you. Why are you a pirate? Why don't you stand with your House?"

The captain shook his head. "No, miss. You have no right to ask me that. We've made our oaths to each other already. I'll keep to myself. But the others? If they accept that exchange, yes. Do you have someone you wish to speak to first?"

She'd thought about asking for Rapsod. To take the chance to beat him senseless. It was probably a bad idea, though. "Well, why not Gjemb?"

"She'll be content to speak to you, I suspect. I'll send her in when we finish supper. She'll be pleased to share your proposal with the other crews as well. Perhaps you'll have a chance to speak to a few before we need to take our next heading."

Madelyn looked down at her wrapped wrist. "I won't have time to learn more about speaking with stone, will I?"

"The iron poisoning won't likely have worn off yet, no. I'm sorry."

"How often will we have to take headings?"

"As we get closer, more often, until we're in sight."

Madelyn swallowed. "I don't like this."

"Neither do I, miss."

She looked up at the captain. "Thank you."

"For what?"

"Guri told me that leaders in Fae don't often care about anyone else, especially not people who aren't theirs. And I'm not yours. But you still care."

"Well, maybe not all of us in Fae are that wicked."

CHAPTER SEVENTEEN

Gjemb stepped into the cabin. Madelyn still sat in the chair by the table.

"Captain said you had something you wanted from me in payment."

Madelyn gestured to the chair across the table from her.

"No, miss. I won't touch the table. I won't tell you what I most want." She showed her teeth a bit as she said it, almost like she was snarling. "I won't give you that power over me."

"Don't touch the table, then," Madelyn said. "I won't either. I just want to get to know you."

"What do you mean?"

"Why are you here? Why are you with Captain Carangth?"

She narrowed her eyes. "Why should I tell you?"

"You owe me for the pain I'm giving for you. This is the price. Tell me your story, and I will release you from your debt."

The fae considered. She glanced at the door she'd come through, at the table, at Madelyn. "I accept your terms." After a moment, she sat. "I come from House Thorn. I budded under the sun and was grown with roots deep in joy." As she spoke, she closed her eyes and lifted her face, as if she was a flower greeting the dawn. "After I was harvested by the House workers, I was placed back in the fields to sing more workers into being."

Madelyn tried to understand. "You were grown?"

"As are all of House Thorn. We have no mothers or fathers. We have vines." She lifted an arm. "Sap runs through our veins to nourish our bodies. I need only the sun and a little water to grow."

Madelyn shook her head. "But you're a person."

"Of course I am!" Gjemb huffed a laugh. "Why wouldn't I be a person simply because I am from House Thorn?"

Madelyn opened her mouth. Then she closed it. "I'm just not used to people being grown on a vine," she finally said. "Here they're born."

The fae shrugged. "Not all plants are born from fruit. Why should all people be born the same way?" She was silent a moment. "I was happy there. I tended the vine. I made sure my sisters were well taken care of. I taught them of our proud House. I harvested them when they were grown. It was enough for me."

"So why did you join Captain Carangth?"

"It was not by choice. When a field is burned, those with roots turn to ash, and those with legs flee." She looked down. "The darkness came. It licked at the edges of our fields. We'd heard how it had struck at House Stone long before. We thought we might be able to survive." She closed her eyes. "We were wrong."

"The darkness?"

Gjemb waved a hand. "Darkness. Weeds of black. They stained the land." She took a shuddering breath. "And my sisters. Their beautiful skin. Their hair. They said they felt no pain, but they were never whole again once the darkness had touched them. The weeds took root in my field. And it was my job to tend to the vines, to our vines. That meant I weeded." Her voice became hard. "And that meant I would destroy this weed."

The walls of the captain's quarters creaked.

145

The fae stood. Small hairs sprouted along her arms and from her cheeks. Her hair budded. "I took a hoe in my hand to uproot the invading darkness."

Madelyn realized the tiny hairs were branches. Gjemb was growing, growing, looking more plant-like every moment. Her hair flowered bright red blossoms. Fruit like grapes hung from her fingers. Her mouth opened, but no sound came out, only the creaking of a tree in the wind.

The walls echoed the sound. The deck beneath her groaned. Every piece of wood in the room seemed to call out in mourning with the fae.

Madelyn stumbled around the table to get to Gjemb.

The fae's skin turned white and thin like a willow's bark. Her mouth snapped shut and open again. "I wasn't enough." Her chin trembled. Her voice grew thick. "I wasn't enough. My vine withered. My beautiful vine. All my sisters. I tried." The petals in her hair drooped. Her locks turned into long pale green leaves.

Madelyn tripped over the roots which had spread over the deck but caught herself on the table. Outside, someone called an alarm. Whatever Gjemb was doing, it was spreading across the ship.

She reached out to the fae with her good hand, touching her rough shoulder. "Gjemb."

"My sisters withered because I wasn't strong enough," she whispered.

She felt guilty because she had failed to rescue those she loved.

Like Madelyn had failed to rescue Renity. Or anyone on the Island.

"I don't know what the dark weeds are," Madelyn said. She tried to find words. "I don't know what it's like to watch someone you love wither. But it's not your fault. You fought for them. You tried so hard."

Gjemb's face became more and more still. The roots continued to spread, tangling around Madelyn's ankles. Vines began climbing her legs.

She didn't move. "Gjemb. Listen to me. Listen to me!" What could she say? She wasn't there. She hadn't seen it. She didn't even know Gjemb. She couldn't say anything that might help.

But she could weep with her. That's all Renity had needed.

And so Madelyn wrapped her arms around Gjemb's form. She simply held her. The vines

147

crept up Madelyn's legs, around her waist, up her back. Leaves flowed from Gjemb's hair and over Madelyn's shoulders. Outside, more cries sounded. Something pounded against the door.

Madelyn held her.

The vines crawled up her arm and along to her elbow. To her wrist.

When they touched the bandages there, the vines stopped. The leaves stopped. The creaking stopped. The groaning stopped.

"Is it true?" Gjemb whispered.

"Yes?" Madelyn asked.

The vines pulled back. The leaves returned into Gjemb's hair. The roots untangled from Madelyn's ankles.

Tears sparkled in the fae's eyes. She touched Madelyn's cheek. She shook her head. "You must stop giving gifts. Not every fae will appreciate it."

"I didn't give any gift."

"No?" She pointed to the table.

An image of the Island floated there. Tiny figures of Grandma, Peter, Renity, and Madelyn poised on the edge, waving. And beside them stood Gjemb. She tended a vine.

"The table shows what you want when you touch it," Gjemb whispered.

Madelyn shook her head. "I don't understand. You were hurting. I was trying to comfort you."

"You didn't run in fear. You didn't tell me to hide my pain. You accepted it. And look. You want to give me a home with you."

Madelyn stared at the image floating above the table. "Gjemb, what happened to your field?"

"It was swallowed by the weeds."

"Do you have a home?"

"Not anymore. Perhaps this ship."

"You're a refugee."

"If you like."

Madelyn nodded. "Then, yes. The Island can be your home. It's a haven." She turned to the fae. "For anyone. *Anyone* who doesn't have a home. Even if they were grown on a vine."

The fae shook her head. She looked almost human again. The door behind her burst open. The captain's eyes were wild. "Gjemb! What happened?"

"I am even more in debt to your Madelyn, Captain. But now, maybe, I don't mind as much." She lifted her chin to Madelyn with a sad smile before turning and leaving.

CHAPTER EIGHTEEN

S he was a refugee. Gjemb was a refugee.

Madelyn sat on the chair beside the table and watched her floating Island. Grandma waved at her. Peter smirked. Renity rolled her eyes. And even little Madelyn stood there, cutlass drawn, smiling toward the sky, daring anyone to come and face her. The tiny feather in the little hat fluttered in an imaginary breeze.

And Gjemb stood nearby, tending a vine.

Imagine that. Imagine if she came back to the Island, how much food they could have. Imagine if she worked with Peter, what they could accomplish for the good of so many others.

And she belonged on the Island. She'd find a home there. Even though she had attacked. Many of the refugees Madelyn had taken in had violent backgrounds, didn't they? Burbin had his knives. Gaershir certainly knew how to fight. Gjemb would fit right in.

But what did that mean?

Did all the pirates belong with them at the Island?

No. No, that couldn't be. They belonged in Fae.

But Peter wasn't trying to go back. And Grandma certainly didn't want to go back. No, the Island was home to them.

So couldn't they welcome a few more refugees from Fae?

The door flew open. Renity stomped over to Madelyn.

Madelyn blinked up at her. "Look. It's the Island."

Renity squinted at the image that floated over the table. "Why are there pirates there?"

Madelyn felt a shock. She turned to look.

Another form had appeared on the Island. Kneeling down, speaking to the stone of the Island, was Guri.

Madelyn realized that she, too, was a refugee. She would belong on the Island just as much. She'd already done more for the Island than anyone else by speaking to the stone and helping the Island stay aloft for even longer.

Madelyn shook her head. "I don't know, Renity. But I'm starting to think about these pirates. They're not what I thought they were."

Renity waited.

"They're here because they don't have homes. At least the ones I've talked to. And that makes them refugees."

"No. No way. Don't you dare."

"But the Island's supposed to be a haven, isn't it? For anyone who doesn't have a home."

Renity glared. "Sure. Anyone who doesn't have a home. And isn't a jerk."

Someone cleared his throat. Captain Carangth stood in the doorway. "Miss. It's time. We need to take another heading."

"Already?" Renity asked.

"Already," Madelyn answered. She stood.

The wind had stilled on the deck. The sun sat crimson on the horizon. The crew watched from around the deck. Gjemb stood beside the stool. Dremit, the fae who put her to sleep, waited on the other side.

Madelyn took her place. Renity hovered nearby. The trunk bloomed again. The captain put on his gloves. He took the blade. He bellowed his orders. Madelyn lifted her right wrist.

The pain was no better this time.

CHAPTER NINETEEN

T he next morning Madelyn woke with both wrists bandaged. Once again, Grandma had not met her in dreams.

Soon Dremit entered the cabin, bearing a platter with more sliced tomatoes on it.

Madelyn clambered out of bed, whimpering as she did. She couldn't use her hands at all without pain. With concentration and bracing herself, she was able to eat the tomatoes. The taste still wasn't great.

Dremit waited nearby.

"Sit down," Madelyn said, nodding toward the other chair the table had made. Her Island had faded, but the chairs remained.

"I only sit when it's time to sleep," she answered. "But Gjemb told us of your offer. And I will repay my debt."

Madelyn nodded, resting her hands in her lap.

"My story is simple. Someone I loved was exiled. I followed."

Madelyn waited for more. Dremit spoke no further, though.

"That's it?"

"Is it enough?"

"Well, I expected more. That sounds like someone talking about a story instead of actually telling the story."

Dremit shook her head. "My domain is dreams, not stories. If you want a story, talk to Rapsod. Or if you want, I will send you a dream that will show you why I am here. But I have tried to protect you. I've kept your sleep dreamless these last nights to aid your healing. It would do you no good to thrash about in your sleep from a dream and harm your wrists even more."

"Oh. That makes sense." She nodded and glanced down at the tomatoes. "You came to the Island to get supplies, right?"

"Of course."

"Why don't you just ask Gjemb to grow food for everyone? She grew some fruit yesterday. I didn't recognize what kind it was, but with how fast she can grow things, why would you ever need supplies?"

Dremit offered a faint smile. "Gjemb does grow us food, but she cannot grow enough. There is too much crew and not enough wood on the ship. It also tires her. We need more than what she and the others from House Thorn can make in this space."

"What if she had more space? Fields and fields?"

"Then I suppose she might be able to do more, but you should ask her." Dremit sighed. "Have I spoken enough? Is my debt repaid?"

"Hm? Oh, yes. I suppose." Madelyn really wanted to know more, but this woman wasn't going to say more, was she?

Dremit nodded once and exited through the door, leaving the tomatoes behind.

And that morning, one after another, the crew came into the captain's quarters to tell their stories.

One woman pushed back against a dark wind until it overwhelmed her and left her without a home. She refused to show any emotion.

One man displeased his lord by refusing to sacrifice his daughter. He and his family were exiled. So, with no land of his own, he signed on with

Captain Carangth to provide a place for his wife and children.

A child ran away to discover adventure and never found his way back home.

More and more came to her, paying for her pain with their stories. And nearly all of them shared pain of their own. And more and more, Madelyn heard tales of standing against an invading darkness and failing. Tales of people losing their homes. Houses going to war and destroying places where they had lived.

Not all of them, but many of the pirates were refugees. They were as homeless as the people from Ebhold who Madelyn had rescued.

And more and more, Madelyn understood that they weren't as ruthless as Peter had made them out to be. Yes, they attacked all the Houses, but they did it to strike at the leaders who were so often corrupt. They did it to protect their families, their loved ones.

And these skyships had become for them a haven, a home to replace the ones they had lost.

Just like the Island was for Madelyn.

And then Rapsod entered. He was still tall, still dashing. He glanced back and forth and sighed.

Madelyn braced herself. This was the one who had hurt her sister so much. But she chose to show courtesy. "What's wrong?" she asked.

"Your friend. The captain thinks it's funny. He's assigned me to watch her. To make sure she's safe. I don't have a moment's peace. She climbs on everything. She's probably getting herself into trouble right now." He draped himself over the chair across from Madelyn. "I hear it told that you look for stories."

"Not just any story. Your story."

"Yes, well. I suppose I could tell you that, but it is not very exciting." He examined his nails. "Are you sure you're interested? I could tell you a better story. Maybe one of a cunning prince who risks everything to save his princess. Or perhaps of a witty rogue with a blade made of griffin's bone who steals the cold from House Frostburn. That one's a favorite in House Cinder, let me tell you!"

"Your story will do nicely, thank you."

"Hm. Well, I suppose it is up to you to set the price and up to me to pay it. As I said, my story is bland and hardly worth the breath to tell it." He sighed. "Well. I was cast out from my House for telling the truth. And that's all there is to it." He made to stand.

"I thought fae couldn't tell lies?"

"Oh, we can't lie, but there's a long space between truth and lies. And when addressing a Queen, well, the truth is a dangerous thing indeed. I found myself exiled. Not just exiled. Hunted. And the Talehunters of House Slumber are dangerous fiends indeed. I sought shelter among the pirates. Captain Carangth has protected me, and I have done my best to plant the seeds of his story wherever I can. It makes our job much easier if people already fear us. They spot the skyships on the horizon and run to hide."

"And you can make people believe your stories."

"Ah, at times."

"Like you made Renity love you."

His smile faded. "Yes. Like I made your friend love me."

"I think she still loves you."

"Yes. But that story has ended. She has no reason to feel anything for me but hate."

"Tell her another story. Break that love."

He looked away. "I've never told such a story. I don't know how."

"Then it's time to learn."

"I have given you your price. You can ask no more unless you pay me something." He stood. "I believe this interview is at an end." He turned to leave.

"Do you love her?" Madelyn asked.

He was facing away from her, so she couldn't read his expression. He lifted his head as if to respond, but simply stood silently. After a moment, he left the captain's quarters, gently shutting the door behind him.

Madelyn shut her eyes.

They all belonged on the Island, didn't they? Even Rapsod. Thoughts rolled around in her head as the wind pushed the skyships ever onward toward the Bridge.

The only one she didn't know about was the captain himself. The one who had gathered them all up into his crews.

So he was the next one she'd have to speak to.

CHAPTER TWENTY

That evening, Carangth himself brought a platter of food for her. This one held a few potatoes chopped up in squares, but raw. Madelyn attempted to eat one of the cubes and spat it out.

"I take it that isn't food, miss?" the captain asked.

"No, the vegetable is food. Potatoes are great. But you need to cook it."

"Oh?"

"Bake it. Mash it up and mix in some cheese. That was always my favorite. There's a hundred ways to eat potatoes, but raw isn't one of them." Madelyn made a face as she looked at the little pile of cubes on her plate.

"Well. Everyone on the crew seems to like it this way well enough." He shrugged and snatched a few squares from her plate. He popped them into his mouth and crunched. "Quite tasty."

She shook her head. "Well, I'm glad you've been giving me tomatoes instead, then."

He shrugged again. "Much of the crew's been coming and going, making their payments. People swinging over from the other ships of my fleet. You've been accepting most of them, I hear."

"I have. But I still don't have your story."

"And you won't get it." He tossed a few more squares into his mouth. "My payment is coming when I leave you and your friend at the Bridge. The deal's already made, miss."

"I thought you might say something like that. I just want to know more about Fae. I don't want to go there. It sounds—well—most of your crew sound like they've been hurt a lot over there."

"Excuse me for saying, miss, but the human realm doesn't sound much better. There's a reason you raised your Island, after all."

She nodded. "I suppose. But everyone here, everyone on your skyship, everyone who's talked to me at least, they all seem to be running from something. And I know what that's like." She looked down at her lap. "I never really fit in. I don't remember Grandma bringing me from Fae, but I remember meeting Renity. She was only a couple years older than I was. She remembered having a little sister who died, so she just adopted me. And we've been together ever since."

"So you know how strong a family not of blood can be. How you can make your own House."

"That tie was the only thing that saved me. Prince Aralane took my grandma. I ran. I hid. And Renity ran with me. She's always been protective of me. I mean, all this was before I knew I was part fae, before I ever talked to stone. But even then, I knew something was wrong. Renity's twenty-two. I'm twenty. But I look . . . Well, I'm still fourteen in every way that matters. Some people even think I still act that way." She rolled her eyes. "And I think that made Renity more protective of me."

"Aye." The captain listened quietly.

"Anyway, Renity ran with me. She had some money, so we were able to buy food for a while. But not for long. We found another village. We moved around for a while. We stole. One time I stole a loaf of bread, but the baker saw me. He chased." She felt her heart quicken just remembering it. "I ran. Oh, I ran so hard. The village was at the foot of these rocky hills, so I ran up one of them. I think the baker was angry because someone dared steal from him. One loaf of bread isn't that much, is it? But he chased me anyway. And when I got to the top of the hill, I didn't know what to do. I didn't have anywhere else to run. I crouched down, like that would keep him from seeing me. It didn't, of course. He kept climbing. So I prayed. I asked to get away. Somehow."

She shook her head. "And the rock listened. It answered my prayer. It lifted up. When the baker saw, he squawked like a chicken and ran away. I thought he was running fast before!"

The captain joined in her laugh.

"But that's how I found out how different I really was. When the rock finally came down and Renity found me, I was sobbing. What kind of monster was I?" She shook her head again. "But she loved me anyway. She held me while I cried. She didn't care that I was so different. I was her sister. And that was enough."

Holding her was enough. Renity didn't do anything to save her. She was just there. Like holding Gjemb was enough. And what Renity had wanted before. Madelyn let that thought linger in her mind.

"Aye." The captain's voice was thoughtful.

"From there, we started figuring out that we could do something more than steal food. We might be able to help other people. But that's a story for another day, I think." Madelyn nodded.

"Aye, I suppose it might be. The time to take another heading comes soon."

"Good." Madelyn stood. "And now you owe me."

"Oh?" Carangth raised an eyebrow.

"Your crew has been paying their debt by telling their stories. And now I've told you mine. I've given you myself. That means you owe me, doesn't it?"

He narrowed his eyes.

"I'm right, and you know it."

"I don't like being in debt to anyone, miss."

"I don't suppose you do. Too bad. You owe me. And you're going to pay."

"You won't get my story." His voice took a dangerous edge. "That will cost far, far more."

"I suppose it would. But I won't ask for that. I have something different to ask." Madelyn leaned forward and tapped the table.

Ripples flowed from her fingers and bounced off the edges of the table. They came back and grew and grew until they formed an image of her Island. Atop it perched little Madelyn, sticking her tongue out at the captain. Grandma stood on one side of her, Peter on the other. Renity hovered behind her.

But Gjemb was there tending her vine, and Guri touching the stone. And Rapsod, standing beside Renity. And many others of Carangth's crew.

"You'll not have my people," he breathed. "They're not possessions to be traded, no matter what the Houses say."

"Good." Madelyn nodded. "I don't want to trade for them. I want to offer them a home. It's in the human realm, but it's a haven. It's a place where they can rest. They're refugees. They're exactly the kind of people I raised the Island for."

"You'd steal my crew." He grew very still, muscles tensed.

"Not steal! I just want to offer them a place to be."

At first, Carangth was so quiet Madelyn wondered if she should explain further. Slowly he relaxed into his typical posture. He rubbed his chin as he stood looking at the Island. "No. You gave me a piece of your past, a small piece. Important, yes, but only a piece of it. You're asking for something much greater. You're asking for those I've bled for. No." It was a solid refusal, but the edge in his voice was dulled.

Madelyn sighed. "I don't want to take them. I just want to offer something to them. To give them a choice."

"You won't." The captain tilted his head as he considered the Island. "Besides, it is too dangerous for us here. We eat raw potatoes. Who knows what else we might eat?"

"If anyone stayed on the Island, we'd teach them how to eat good potatoes."

"Aye, I suppose you would. But they're my crew, and I won't give them up. But"—he raised a finger—"allow me to offer something else in exchange for your story." He tapped his finger on the table's surface.

Once more, the ripples spread out. They climbed the Island. They marred little Madelyn's features. They shook through Peter and Gjemb and the rest.

And the ripples spread out past the Island. The image shifted and changed.

Piers came out from the Island. Skyships docked there. Fae moved back and forth from the ships to the village on the Island.

"I won't give up my crew. But what if you offered us a haven, as you say? A place to dock. A place of safety away from the Houses that hunt us. We'll pay, of course. You need more food. Maybe Gjemb can do more on your Island than she can do here. So you won't be a place for us to raid. You'll be a place for us to find friends. A port in a storm."

Madelyn took in the image and the words. She considered the counteroffer.

"Yes," she said. She didn't have to think anymore. It was a way for everyone to win. The Island would get more food and more friends. And the pirates would have a place to rest. "Yes."

"Well, then. We'll find the Bridge and chart our course better this time so we can find our way back to you. Miss, I do believe we have the beginning of a good partnership. But for now, I'm sorry. It's time to take a new heading." He extended his hand to her. "Come on, then, lass. It's time."

CHAPTER TWENTY-ONE

The next days were a mixture of stories and pain. Madelyn decided to spend as much time as she could on the deck, feeling the wind in her face. Many of the pirates found her there to tell their tales. Pirates who had been born to House Grave, House Beast, House Hunger, and many others shared their stories. None of them were overwhelmed as much as Gjemb had been, but many grew emotional.

"Our forests wilted. Our prey no longer ran. How can a wolf hunt prey that simply lies and accepts the death you bring?" The hairy fae shook his head. "We had to find other places to hunt. And the last time I went back, I could not find my forest at all. I think it has been swallowed."

"By what?" Madelyn asked.

"By darkness."

Later, a well-dressed man stood beside Madelyn, gazing out at the clouds. "They remind me of home. These are far cleaner, of course. I grew up in the factories. Made myself something. Only House Cobble has that. A way for a coalkin to become a gearer."

"I have no idea what you're talking about," Madelyn said.

"Of course. I apologize. Our worlds are very different, aren't they? But there is a kind of charm to this place. Quaint."

Guri visited. "Your iron poisoning isn't going away."

"It's not."

"I'd like to teach you how to speak to stone."

"I'd like that too."

Guri crossed her arms. Her long cloak trailed behind her on the deck of the ship. "There has to be something we can do."

"Are you really thirty?" Madelyn asked.

"Yeah. I look old for my age."

She shook her head. "I don't understand. I'd hate to be as young as you look for that long. I don't like being this young now! I want to grow up. I should be grown up."

Guri shrugged. "Well, you are what you are. Why complain? Just enjoy what you can. Like running."

Madelyn tilted her head.

"Just run. Feel your feet against the stone. Speak to it through your toes. Laugh, and let the stone laugh with you. Run, and let the stone race with you." She paused. "And if you run fast enough, maybe you can outrun your own feelings. Forget everyone who ran away from you."

Gjemb visited too. "Thank you."

"For what?"

"You held me. I believe the last time I was held was the day I was plucked from the vine. I held many of my sisters, of course, as they grew." She stood silently for a while. "I have not mourned for them well. I wish I could have taken them to House Grave to be taken care of. To be placed on the graves of others so they could honor each other."

"I have a friend from House Grave. Would it help to talk to him? He might know some way to help."

"Perhaps. I have friends from House Grave here. Crewmates."

"Would it help to talk to them?"

"Perhaps. Madelyn of the Sky, you continue to give of yourself. Be careful, or there will be nothing left to give."

Madelyn shrugged. "I'm pretty sure there's plenty left."

Gjemb glanced at the bandages around her arms. "Somehow I doubt that."

Later, Rapsod himself approached. "What notes do you sing tonight?" he asked.

Madelyn glanced around. "I'm not singing."

"Everyone sings. Everyone. And everyone dances. You only need to stop and listen to hear it." He lifted his face to the wind and breathed deeply. "I hear a sadness in your song, but your dance is bright."

"What do you want?"

He considered. He glanced down at his feet and then back to the deck behind him. No one was nearby. "I would ask a favor. You may set your price on it should we strike a deal."

Madelyn attempted to cross her arms, but her wounds burned when she put pressure on them. She settled for leaving her arms at her sides. "What do you want?"

"Your friend. Ah, well. Your friend danced. She didn't dance like any woman I met in any port nor from any House." He looked far, far away. "I want to dance with her again. I won't sing. I won't enchant her. But there is something about her."

"And you want me to talk to her?"

"I suspect you have a certain power over her."

Madelyn glanced around before focusing on Rapsod again. "Why should I bother doing anything for you? You're the one who enchanted her. It's your fault she's here. I should be furious at you for doing that to my friend."

"It's all my fault." He spoke the words flippantly, throwing his hand into the air. But then he stopped himself. "Yes. It is my fault. Forgive me." He smoothed his hands over his open vest. "House Slumber is not known for speaking the truth plainly, and the one time I did, I was exiled. So let me try." He composed himself and focused fully on Madelyn. "It is my fault. I have offended her. She has every reason to be furious with me, as do you. I wronged you. Deeply." He closed his eyes. "I owe her a great deal."

"And you want to go more in debt?"

"To dance with her again? Yes. It would be worth it."

"That's right. You owe me."

Renity's voice made Rapsod jump. He whirled to face her. "How long have you been eavesdropping?"

"Long enough." She crossed her arms and narrowed her eyes. "And you do owe me. For doing all that. For singing and making me fall in love with you. So you should be coming to me."

He blushed and looked away. "My lady, it wouldn't be proper for someone to approach another he has wronged so deeply."

"Nope. Probably not. But here we are. You owe me. And I've been thinking this over. You know how many boys came my way only to leave again? You know how many of them refused to dance with me? They thought I was too loud or too silly or too attached to Madelyn."

"Your loudness enchants me."

"Right. So this is what you're going to do if you really want to pay your debt." She drew her rapier. "You're going to dance with me."

"My lady?"

She lunged.

Rapsod scurried out of the way. Madelyn laughed. Renity winked at her. She called after Rapsod, "By the time we finish our dance, you'll be dead, I'll be dead, or we'll be kissing!"

Now he joined her laugh. He drew the rapier at his side and met her, steel for steel.

The pirates on deck stopped what they were doing to watch. The captain put his fists on his hips and laughed. Madelyn grinned.

And when they were done dancing, Renity kissed Rapsod.

Madelyn blushed.

CHAPTER TWENTY-TWO

"Y ou can't keep doing this." Renity sat on the edge of Madelyn's bed.

It had been almost a week since Renity had danced with Rapsod. Now Madelyn rarely saw her. She was told the two of them scurried off to private places in the skyship or even swung to visit other ships.

And of course, the captain had taken other headings. Now Madelyn had bandages over both wrists, both ankles, and a bandage around her left calf. She couldn't walk without help.

"The captain says he thinks we're close," Madelyn said. "And my wrists are almost healed."

"It doesn't matter, does it?" Renity took one of her hands. "If you weren't hurting so much, I'd whack you. Madelyn, it doesn't matter if the pirates are good or not. It doesn't matter that you made a deal with the captain." She closed her eyes. "You need to stop this."

Madelyn squeezed Renity's hand. "I will. Once we're at the Bridge."

"And once they drop us off, what're you going to do? You can't walk anywhere. We don't have money to hire a wagon. We don't have pigeons to send to Grandma. We'll be stuck there. And if you think I can hunt to find us food, you're as foolish as Grandma says."

"I can dream at Grandma. Even with iron poisoning."

"Really? Then why haven't you been? Oh, don't give me that look. If you'd been talking with her, you would have told me. You'd say that we didn't have to be scared. You'd tell me that she made a deal with flying rabbits that were going to attack the skyships and free us, and then the pirates would all have to beg for mercy."

Madelyn huffed a light laugh. "Grandma hasn't talked to me for a long time. Not since our first night here."

"What did she say?"

"That she'd meet us at the Bridge."

Renity sat silently for a while. "She's coming?"

"She said she was."

"She's going to be angry."

"I imagine."

Renity looked toward the door and past it toward the deck and those who stood on it. "She's going to be angry at the pirates."

"I know."

"Are you going to tell them?"

Madelyn worried the hem of her shirt. "I'm hoping we're traveling fast enough that it won't matter. I mean, we're in skyships, right? They have to be going faster than anyone on land. They'll drop us off and be on their way. And then Grandma will find us and bring us home."

"What will she think if Rapsod's with us?"

Madelyn frowned. "He won't be, so it won't matter."

"Madelyn, he's coming home with us. Or I'm going with him." She looked back at Madelyn. "Don't. I know what you're going to say. We're not separating." Renity squeezed her hand. "Just be happy for me, all right?" She looked down and then back up. She almost glowed. "The captain's going to marry us."

Madelyn gasped. "What?"

"It's true. On the Bridge. Right there, at the connection between fae and human lands."

Now Madelyn really had no words. Married? But Renity was her big sister! She wasn't allowed to get married! Why would she do that? She was happy being by herself! Some women were meant to be married, and others were meant to whack you upside the head. Renity was meant to whack you upside the head!

"Be happy. Please. We were going to surprise you. Rapsod said it was your fault, anyway. He wasn't going to marry me. He was just going to leave me behind, except you had to talk to him." She poked Madelyn in the shoulder.

"My fault? What did I do?"

"You asked him if he loved me. Until then, he was just annoyed he couldn't fly away. Usually, he charms a girl and leaves. But this time he was stuck with me, until we got to the Bridge at least. But when you asked him, he had to think about it." Her smile grew. "He says he likes dancing with me. That dancing with a human girl is more, is different than any fae he's ever danced with. And he says—" She blushed. "He says I'm more beautiful than the seventeen fae Queens."

"How many fae Queens are there?"

"Does it matter?" She giggled. "Madelyn, you've been there. You know how many men only wanted to be with me because they thought I would clean up after them or because they thought I could cook for them. None of them liked that I could dance or that I could climb. Rapsod dared me to climb the sail wings. And you know what? I did. I went out farther than he did."

"He likes that you climb?"

"He does!"

Madelyn shook her head. Renity had had crushes before, of course. And a few men had pursued her. A few had even been serious, but none of them seemed to like how she was so sure of herself. But if Rapsod really did love her . . .

And if Renity really was going to get married, if Rapsod was going to marry her . . . Well, maybe it wasn't so bad. "So . . . So, now what?" Madelyn asked. "Are you really going to stay on the skyship?"

"The captain keeps calling me *miss*, so he doesn't think so. And now, with this deal you and the captain have worked out, maybe Rapsod would be fine on the Island. He could still see his friends. We still need to work it out."

"You're really going to get married."

"Yeah." Renity glowed. "Someone loves me for me. Not to trick me. Not to get anything. Just because I dance with him and he dances with me."

"And you forgave him? For, you know, casting a spell on you?"

Her gaze became distant. "We worked it out. He'll be paying for that for a while. But he promised to never do it again. And besides," she said as she grinned, "if he hadn't done that, we wouldn't be here now. So it worked out for good, I guess."

"Well." Madelyn sighed. "You're going to need someone to stand with you at the ceremony."

Renity gave her a light punch on the shoulder. "You better! I'm not going to ask Gjemb or anyone else to stand with me! It's gotta be my sister."

"So we need to get to the Bridge fast," Madelyn said, "so you can be married before Grandma gets there."

And now Renity drooped. "Yeah."

"Which means they need to take a heading."

She nodded.

"Which means I want to even more. So you can have your wedding."

"You're going to make my wedding the saddest day of my life, aren't you? Having to hear you scream like that again."

"It's my wedding gift, then. Since I can't get you anything else, I'll get you to the Bridge on time." Madelyn tried to sit up in the bed and failed. Her wrists and ankles screamed at her. "Help me out of bed. Let's see if they need to take a heading again. Tell the captain we need to get there faster."

"You don't have to do this."

"If you don't help me, I'll just fall onto the deck and squirm all the way to the door."

"You would, too."

"You know I would."

Renity closed her eyes. "Madelyn, I don't deserve a friend like you."

"You're right. You deserve someone way better. Now help me get out of bed, you big dummy."

CHAPTER TWENTY-THREE

Captain Carangth was happy to hurry. He had ordered Stuhi to go easy on the wind to give Madelyn more time to recover between each heading. Now though, at Madelyn's urging, he told Stuhi to call on the winds more and more.

Madelyn spent even more time on the deck. She was in pain, yes, but it was better to be in the open air. Besides, it was fun to watch Renity and Rapsod out on the sail wings. Now that they were hurrying to their wedding, the two didn't feel the need to scurry away anymore. They danced over the fabric and across the wooden struts. They laughed together and fell into each other's arms.

"They are happy, aren't they?" Madelyn asked as she leaned against the rail.

"Aye," answered Captain Carangth.

"Will you actually marry them?"

"It's one of the best joys of being a captain. Why wouldn't I?"

"Does he actually love her?"

The captain gave a hearty laugh. "I've known Rapsod for years. He's never allowed a woman onto the ship. He's made sure to never come close to flirting with any of the crew unless they knew he wasn't actually interested. This is the first time a woman's chased him. I think he likes being chased. Once he got over how strange a human woman can be."

Madelyn shook her head. "I hope we get there soon enough."

"Aye, lass. Me too."

Madelyn opened her mouth to tell him about Grandma, but no. Stuhi's winds were faster than anyone on land could be. Instead she said, "You called me lass before."

"I did. It was no mistake."

"But I'm not a member of your crew."

"Well, maybe not. But you've aided my crew so much." He turned and leaned against the rail. "We'd wandered far from the Bridge, it seems. But now you've given us hope of getting home. You've given yourself. You're not just someone we kidnapped. Not anymore." He turned serious. "And

183

if I allowed you to make that offer, I think many of the crew would stay with you on the Island. My fleet might be halved. Or worse. Other than me, no one has ever sacrificed for them."

"Then I'm glad we've worked out a way to help everyone."

He nodded.

"Will you take Renity with you? Or will Rapsod stay with her?"

"Oh? I wasn't aware either would happen."

Madelyn frowned. "But they'll be married."

"Aye."

"So they should be together."

"You humans have such strange ideas. When a sailor goes to sea, is his wife always with him?"

"I don't know. I grew up far from the shore."

"Aye. You did at that. But sailors and their husbands or wives are often parted for seasons, sometimes years, at a time. It makes one yearn for the other, and their reunions are the most joyful things under the sun." His eyes shone. "So when we visit your Island, Renity will see her husband. And they'll find great joy, I wager."

"It'll be hard."

"Nothing in life is worth anything unless it's hard. Like protecting refugees. If it were easy, would you fight so hard to protect them?"

Madelyn shook her head.

"Lass, there's something I want you to have. Walk with me."

He offered his arm. Madelyn accepted it and limped with him to the stool that still stood in the center of the deck.

"Gjemb!" the captain called.

She came from somewhere belowdecks. "Captain?"

"Bring the blades out."

"But we don't need to take a heading. Not yet."

"We won't be taking a heading. Bring the blades."

"Aye."

And the chest bloomed again.

"Gjemb, grow vines around the hilt. Tight."

She nodded. "I think I see, Captain." She closed her eyes and did the work commanded her.

Blades are often solid pieces of metal, and these iron cutlasses were no different. The hilts of many blades are wrapped with cloth or leather to soften the place where they're held. Now this hilt was tightly wrapped with soft green leaves.

The captain didn't put on his gloves. He reached down and took hold of the hilt. He hissed. "Still stings," he said. "Here. I think you might find this easier to hold."

Madelyn took the hilt from him. She didn't even feel a tingle. Her half-human blood protected her as long as there wasn't direct contact between her skin and the iron.

"Lass, if you stand with us, if other fae follow us from our lands, you may have need of an iron cutlass. One of your men had iron hammers, I saw. Good. You may need something even more. And I noticed you lost your cutlass in your escape attempt. So here. To repay you for the blade you lost."

The weight pulled at Madelyn's wrist uncomfortably because of her injuries, but the hilt felt right in her hand. She swung it a few times. The balance was exquisite. She could fight and fight well with it.

"Thank you," she said.

"Aye. Just repaying a debt." He glanced up. "Gjemb, seal up the trunk again. We don't need those flying around."

"Aye, Captain," she said.

The trunk closed like a flower at sunset.

"Won't we need to take another heading again soon anyway?" Madelyn asked as she sheathed her new blade.

"No." He grinned. "The last time we took a heading, we were able to get the exact position. Stuhi! Take us down!"

"Aye!" the fae answered. Soon, the skyships turned downward.

"Rapsod! Renity! You fools get back in the ship!"

Both began clambering back over the sails.

A few wisps of cloud spun by, and then more. A fog absorbed the skyships.

"By our heading, we should be over the Bridge soon. We'll drop low enough for our little ceremony on the Bridge, and then we'll be off, back to Fae. We'll see you soon enough, though." The captain grinned.

Madelyn held her breath.

They were so close. If they beat Grandma and whoever she brought with, the pirates could return home, and she could do whatever was necessary to convince those on the Island that the pirates were friends. And a skyship had to travel more quickly than Grandma could, right? There was no way she could get here faster.

Then again, Grandma did know the route already. And Grandma being Grandma, she probably knew some way to travel more quickly.

No. It was impossible. They'd be fine. Renity and Rapsod would be wed. And that'd mean the pirates would have to come back. And then Gjemb would help the Island grow food. And Guri could teach her about speaking to stone. And Madelyn could provide a haven for any of them. For all of them.

The clouds cleared. Below them lay an ancient, rotting village. Before them lay a marsh and a lake. A long, long Bridge of stone and wood led across it into impossibly dense mist.

Madelyn couldn't see anyone.

"All stop!" the captain bellowed.

"All stop!" the pilots from all the ships answered.

"Guri, if you would, lass." The captain nodded to the cloaked girl.

She raised a hand and spoke with the stone. Soon they began to descend to the Bridge.

Renity's fingers entwined with Rapsod's. He grinned down at her. She lifted her face to his. They kissed.

Madelyn made retching noises.

Renity stuck her tongue out at her.

This was it. They'd make it. Madelyn let out a shaky breath.

"Captain!"

Madelyn didn't know who called out, but she felt the danger. A heavy weight seemed to push down on her heart.

The lines holding the ship to the stones disintegrated. Madelyn watched it all happen, her thoughts moving faster than a hummingbird. The strands of the cords sundered, one by one, as if they were ancient. The vines that Gjemb had grown withered and turned to dust. The tarp was loosed from the ship. The rocks floated up, up, into the cloudy sky.

Gravity wrapped its fingers around the skyship. The deck tipped forward. Madelyn clung to the rail. Renity screamed. The captain muttered words that Grandma would yell at him for. The view went from the horizon to the marsh.

The bow impacted the water. Towering waves shot up on either side. Huge cracks sounded as the sail wings shattered against the surface of the water. Everyone fell to the deck. The boat shuddered and moaned under the pressure.

Madelyn's entire side shouted pain. Her wrists, her ankles, various parts of her legs, all the parts of her that had been touched by iron screamed.

She didn't have time to deal with any of that. She got up, drawing the iron cutlass.

"Report!" the captain bellowed as he struggled back to his feet.

"Captain Carangth. You've taken someone very dear to me." The familiar voice thundered over the waters. Madelyn looked over to the Bridge. A single stooped figure with white braids stood there. "And you'll return her. Now."

Chapter Twenty-Four

The other skyships circled above. Madelyn felt rather than saw a drawing in of energy. The crews on those ships were ready to rain down fire on Grandma.

Before they could loose anything, though, the water off to the side of their ship bubbled. A huge rocky fist rose from the marsh, dripping water and reeds. It was large enough to crash onto the boat and shatter it to kindling.

"Tell your friends up there to stay away if they want to see you alive," Grandma shouted from where she stood on the Bridge. She sounded so, so certain and dangerously calm.

The captain raised a trembling fist and looked up at the other ships of his fleet.

They continued to circle, but something eased in the pressure around them.

"Good. You're not a complete idiot. Now. Return my granddaughter and her friend."

Renity stumbled to her feet. Rapsod still struggled to stand. She reached down and pulled him up. She supported him, looking defiantly back toward the Bridge.

Madelyn braced herself at the rail facing the Bridge. She couldn't move far at all, but she should still be able to speak. "Grandma. We can talk. We've figured out a deal."

"Oh, no, Granddaughter. We do not make deals with the fae. Come here." Stones rose from under the water, forming a path to the Bridge. Twenty yards of rocks led to the low railing that protected the Bridge. Not far at all. On a good day, Madelyn could have dashed across if she wanted.

It was not a good day, though. And she didn't want to cross. Not to that woman. Not right now. She knew what Grandma was like when she was angry. She wasn't a person then. She was a force of nature. Madelyn should have known. Of course Grandma was going to get here first. And of course she wouldn't listen.

Captain Carangth stood next to Madelyn. His fingers dug into her shoulder as he stared across the stones toward Grandma. "Lass. That's your grandma?"

"Yeah," she answered.

He swore. And then he swore again. He swore a whole lot.

From across the water, the old woman said, "I would kindly ask you to not use such language in front of my granddaughter. She is innocent, and I would not want you to influence her."

"What's wrong?" Madelyn asked without turning toward the captain.

"Lass, that's the Lost Queen. She sat upon the Stone Throne." His voice shook. "She doesn't need an army to destroy my fleet. She can do it all on her own."

"The Lost Queen? That's just my grandma. She's no queen." Madelyn gazed over the waters at the woman who had raised her, who had taught her to care for all around, even as she spoke with harsh love. This was the woman who had taught so many wisewomen how to tend wounds and bind up the broken. She didn't belong with the rulers of the Fae, not from what the crew had taught her about the fae realm! Her anger was legendary, but only at fools.

"No, lass. That woman isn't *just* anything."

Madelyn shook her head. If Grandma was some queen, that made her royalty too. And she was never royalty.

Then again, she didn't know she was half fae until a few months ago. Grandma had kept the truth from her before, hadn't she?

"I'm afraid the captain is correct, Granddaughter," Grandma called from the Bridge. "Something I didn't want you to know. Those who know they are descended from royalty can be such bothers, can't they, Captain?"

"I'd rather not say," Carangth answered.

"Of course not. You didn't tell her your story, did you? It would so ruin your mystique. But for now, I want my granddaughter back. And her friend, I suppose."

Madelyn swiveled to face the captain. She whispered, "If you let us go, you can come back to the Island, right?"

The tall fae eyed the old woman on the Bridge. "We know the way now, yes, but that doesn't mean we'll be welcome. She holds sway there, I'm guessing. And if she does, we'll never be welcome."

Madelyn narrowed her eyes. "We'll see. I can be very persuasive."

"So can she."

Madelyn glanced at Renity. She held Rapsod's hand so hard it trembled. Their knuckles were white.

"I made a promise," Madelyn said. "And so did Renity. If they're not wed today, it'll have to be soon, won't it? Can't have anyone breaking any promises."

Carangth's eyes lit up. "Aye, lass. Aye. Can't have that." He glanced back at Renity and Rapsod. "Madelyn, maybe you don't know this. Fae have a thing about oaths. We're bound to keep them. If we don't, our very blood betrays us. We have funny ways to work around that, with how we word things or what we leave out. But the Bridge . . ." A grin crept across his face. "The Bridge. Legends say that anyone who makes a vow there is bound forever. It's not just their blood. All of creation works to make sure those oaths are kept. And if we can get Renity and Rapsod onto the Bridge, if I can wed them there, the promise will bind my crews and your people together. The Bridge will see to that."

Madelyn's grin matched his. "Why didn't you tell me sooner?" She turned to Grandma. "Grandma, I made a promise to the captain and the crew that I'd bring them safely to the Bridge. And then I made another oath. They'll receive safe harbor at the Island. I made a promise, Grandma."

"I see." She was silent for a moment. "Well, then. There's a reason I said to not make any oaths to the fae. They're tricky."

"Yes you are," she answered.

"If you were here, I'd whack you. But since you're over there and captured by pirates, well, I think it's time you just came home. Now, cross to the Bridge, please."

The stone fist on the other side of the ship flexed its fingers, dripping stagnant marsh water and clumps of reeds.

"Renity, help me down, please." Madelyn tugged at the brim of her hat.

Madelyn's friend came to her side and helped her climb over the rail and slide down to the stone pathway. Then she clambered over too and soon stood beside her.

"How are we getting Rapsod onto the Bridge?" Renity whispered.

"I have no idea. But Grandma's not waiting anymore," Madelyn whispered back. She leaned on her friend and limped along, wincing with every step. Their going was very slow.

About ten feet from the ship, Madelyn stopped. "Wait. The lines holding the ship to the stones. They disintegrated." She looked up at Grandma. "Where's Peter?"

"Your friend? Oh, he's been very helpful."

"Promise me, Grandma. Promise me you'll let Captain Carangth and his crews go. That you'll not hurt them."

"Oh, I swear that I will do no further harm to any of those pirates. Happy, Granddaughter?"

Madelyn eyed the Bridge. Where was Peter? He had to be here. He always wanted to save her, to keep an eye on her. He must have gone insane when she was taken and he was left behind. And he had to be close to have worked his magic on the skyship.

She leaned on Renity and continued the long, limping walk to the Bridge. It stood right on the water, more like a dock or a pier than a bridge. As they came closer, only a simple rail, about waist-high, separated Madelyn from her grandma.

"Come here, Granddaughter." She reached out to Madelyn.

She allowed Grandma to help her over the rail. Renity followed as soon as Madelyn had made it over.

"Well. It appears the pirates mistreated you badly. Look at all those bandages." She frowned deeply. "They need to pay. No one harms my granddaughter."

"You promised not to hurt them."

"I did. But they didn't." She nodded her head toward the mist-shrouded end of the Bridge.

Forms appeared in the mist: men in armor with blue uniforms underneath. Kenevir's military. At the line's head marched Prince Aralane. At his side strode Peter Grave.

He grinned widely at Madelyn. "We've come to save you!"

CHAPTER TWENTY-FIVE

Madelyn had a very uncomfortable urge to throw her arms around Peter. Instead, she scowled. "I didn't need saving!"

"That's what you always say." He rushed forward and threw his arms around her.

She collapsed from the pain. She cried out.

"What did they do to you?" Madelyn had never heard such anger in his voice. He turned to the ship that lay in the marsh. "Houseless pirates!" he snarled.

Grandma waved a few fingers. More stones rose from the marsh, providing additional paths for the Kenevir forces to get to the ship.

"You said you wouldn't harm them!"

"I did. But fae are tricky. Haven't you learned that yet?" Grandma gave her a cold glance.

"Only from you!"

"Apparently not enough." She turned away, dismissing her. "Prince Aralane, here are the pirates who kidnapped the girl who rescued your kingdom. I won't move against them. I've made a promise."

The prince glanced at Madelyn. "That looks worse than what my brother did to her."

"Far worse. She has iron poisoning."

He turned toward the ship. "Grave, what's our best attack?"

"Send your troops over. I'll do everything I can to make sure anything they use against you falls apart."

"Sounds good to me. Kenevir! Attack!"

The men bounded over the rail and onto the rock paths. They pounded across, swords raised.

Madelyn yelled, "No!"

"They must pay," Grandma said.

"Do you really think they have anything to be scared of?" Renity snapped. "They handled everyone on the Island easily. Sure, these Kenevir guys can fight, but what'll they do against fae?"

"What indeed?"

Madelyn's eyes widened. "No." Darkness coiled in her gut.

"What's wrong?" Renity asked.

"The swords. I couldn't feel it before because of the iron poisoning, but they're not normal swords. They're made from iron."

On the deck of the skyship, Gjemb waved her hands. Reeds grew from the marsh along the stone paths and dripped over them. They wound around the soldiers' legs. Men hacked at the plants with their swords, still screaming their battle cries. Aralane shouted, "Grave!"

"On it!" yelled Peter. He grunted with the effort. A wave seemed to pass through the plants like a strange wind. And wherever the wind touched, reeds turned brown and brittle.

The soldiers soon passed through this first obstacle, roaring toward the ship.

Now Guri stepped up. She spoke with the stone paths. They shook. Water began to burble over the edges. The soldiers splashed through puddles. Even from here, Madelyn could see the effort on her face.

"None of that," Grandma said, absently waving a hand. The paths stood firm.

And then Guri smiled. Stone began to fall from the sky, pelting the soldiers. Rocks the size of fists pummeled them.

201

Madelyn grinned. It'd been a distraction. She made Grandma think the paths were the focus while she was lifting the stones into position. That's why she had to concentrate so much.

She searched the ship. She couldn't spot the captain, nor Rapsod.

Good. That meant they were making their way to the Bridge, out of sight, probably wading through the muck of the marsh out in the fog.

She turned to Grandma. "Can't you see? They could be hurting the soldiers so much more. They could have killed us on the Island if they wanted. They don't want to! They just want to get home. That's why they took me! And once I knew that, I gave myself willingly."

"Granddaughter. They took something of mine. They'll pay."

"Is that all I am to you? Just something you own? Not even someone you love?" Madelyn shook her head. "Carangth's right. You're just a Queen from over there, aren't you? Selfish and petty. Someone who only cares about how much she owns."

"None of that, Granddaughter. I take what is due me. We'll address it when we get home."

"You always say that! But you never actually address anything!" Madelyn's hands twitched. This was stupid. Grandma wasn't even listening.

She had to do something. She still couldn't talk to stone. Even if she could, Grandma was so much more powerful. But she had her iron cutlass, didn't she? Did she dare use it?

She looked at her grandma. She didn't see the soldiers reach the boat. She didn't watch their iron blades slice through anything the fae lifted to protect themselves. She didn't hear the screams nor smell the sizzling of skin.

She only saw an old woman who refused to listen to anyone. A woman she loved, but who had turned bitter, who refused to care for people as she should. As she always had before.

Anger kindled in Madelyn's heart. This was her grandma. Grandma was supposed to be good. She might not always be nice, no, but she loved. She loved with a fierceness that would burn down mountains. She longed to learn more, even if it was from her granddaughter.

Madelyn's hand twitched against the hilt Gjemb had wrapped for her.

On the deck of the skyship, Gjemb raised a hedge to separate the soldiers from the fae. Thick thorns kept them apart. The men hacked at the hedge. It wouldn't stand long. Guri stood beside Gjemb. A black mark sizzled on her cheek. She couldn't speak with stone. Behind them all, the stone fist loomed. Grandma had said she wouldn't attack. She was keeping her promise.

But Madelyn hadn't made any promises, had she? Not to Grandma.

Her muscles burned, but they obeyed. She lifted her iron cutlass. She stepped forward on shaking legs. She pointed the tip of her blade at Grandma's neck.

The old woman turned and raised an eyebrow. "Really, Granddaughter? Do you think you could hurt me?"

"No. I can't." She shook her head. "I don't want to. But you need to end this. They let Renity and me go. That was their plan. The captain made an oath to let us go."

Grandma rolled her eyes. "And then what? We let them go? And the next time someone wants to kidnap you, they think they can get away with it. That you'll play nice. No. We need to send a message. Don't worry. We won't touch those other skyships unless they come down here. And their captain gave them an order not to, so we should be safe." She didn't even glance at the blade aimed at her.

"Grandma. Please. Tell the men there's been a mistake. Tell them to draw back."

"I can't," she said. "They're under Aralane's command, not mine."

"He'll listen to you. You know he will."

"Granddaughter, I carried you from Fae to our home in Kenevir. Do you truly think I would allow anyone to take you from me?"

"I can save myself now. I'm not a baby anymore."

She laughed. Grandma laughed at her! "Really? You have no idea. You are so, so young. No. I know better than you, and this proves it. You're not ready for leadership. You don't know who to trust. I'll tell Aralane he'll have to muddle on without my counsel. Clearly, you need me on the Island. Then you can go play with your childish friends if you want."

"Maybe I'm a child compared to you, but I'm a child with a sword." She stepped closer. The blade hovered inches from Grandma's face.

"You are making me angry, Granddaughter."

The fire inside her turned cold. "My name is Madelyn. Call me that."

"When you've earned a name, I'll call you by name."

Madelyn leaned forward. That's all she did. The blade moved forward just an inch. Its tip grazed Grandma's cheek.

She flinched back. "Ungrateful child! I've done all this for you!" Her hands flew to her face. A wisp of smoke rose from her cheek. "I sacrifice everything, my throne, for you, and you do this? I've given you everything! Everything!" She clenched a fist.

Nothing happened.

"You poisoned me," she whispered. She clenched her fist again.

Her eyes darted to the marsh, to the stone fist, and then back to her own fist. "You poisoned me," she whispered, almost to herself this time. Her attention snapped to Madelyn. "Again. Madelyn, you need to poison me again. Longer."

Madelyn stumbled back a step. "Excuse me?"

"Granddaughter." Her voice regained its edge. "You dare strike me? I sat on the Stone Throne. None may touch me and live!" Her voice grew more ragged as she spoke. Something in her eyes changed.

Madelyn pushed forward again. Grandma dodged this time. "Drop your weapon, child," she snarled.

Madelyn kept the blade between them. What was going on?

At the ship, men drooped as Dremit worked her magic on them. They clutched their iron swords, though, and that protected them. Gjemb did her best to grow more vines to stop them. Other fae had jumped from the ship and tried to wade to safety in the marsh water. Soldiers leaped after them. Aralane stood over Guri, his blade raised to strike her down. Peter raced here and there, doing his best to protect the soldiers and decay the fae defenses. Men screamed. Fae screamed.

Madelyn hurt so much. She shook her head. She didn't have time for pain. They hurt more.

She swung her cutlass. Grandma stepped back. She raised her fist. The fist over the boat creaked. "Granddaughter, stop, or I will slam my fist into the boat. Everyone will die. Everyone."

The Bridge glowed underneath Grandma, as if in warning.

"I don't know who you are, but you're not my Grandma." Madelyn's cutlass graced Grandma's raised arm. The stone fist froze in place.

"Good, Madelyn. Keep going. The iron is working." Grandma's voice was soft, familiar.

Madelyn blinked. "Grandma?"

"No. You may address me as Queen, child."

No. That didn't sound like Grandma at all. But it had for a moment.

"No. No one so weak as you could be my family. You do not belong to any House I would rule." Her eyes burned.

And tears clouded Madelyn's vision. "Fine." She swung her blade hard.

Grandma dodged. She stepped aside. Back. Madelyn couldn't touch her. Her legs screamed in pain. Her wrist would give out soon. Still she fought on.

Would she do this? Would she actually hurt her grandma, whatever had happened to her?

She didn't have time to think about it. Fae were going to die, if they hadn't died already. Soldiers were going to die. Whatever had happened to her grandma had to stop.

The iron cutlass wove through the air, faster, faster. Grandma laughed as she danced away from it.

And then she backed up into a solid form. Hands landed heavily on her shoulders. She snarled as she fought against the grip.

"Lass," Captain Carangth said, "do what you must. I would see you go home free." His red coat dripped mud from the marsh. Behind him stood Rapsod, just as muddy.

"No! You wouldn't hurt your grandma, would you?" Her snarls turned to pleading.

"You're not my grandma," Madelyn said. She lunged.

CHAPTER TWENTY-SIX

M adelyn slapped the flat edge of the blade against Grandma's cheek.

Grandma wailed. Her body trembled. Her hands clenched into fists and spasmed back open. Whisps of smoke rose where the metal touched her skin. Madelyn smelled charred flesh. Tears flowed from Grandma's eyes.

They fell from Madelyn's, too.

Finally, she pulled the blade back. Grandma fell limp in Carangth's arms. He gently laid her down. She whimpered.

And then Madelyn realized how quiet it was. The fighting on the ship had stopped. Everyone had turned toward the Bridge.

"Aralane! Peter! Call off the attack!" Madelyn called over the water.

The prince strode to the ship's rail. "Madelyn! We have them on the run!"

"Only because they don't want to actually hurt you! They could make you fall asleep or wrap you in thorns with a thought. Do you really think you're more powerful than that?"

Aralane glanced behind him. In the brief moment it took him to do so, vines snaked around his legs and bound his hands to the ship's rail.

"If they wanted to hurt you, you'd be far worse off," Madelyn said.

"She's right. You've fought enough," Captain Carangth said. "Why not sheathe your sword and join us on the Bridge for a celebration? We need spill no more blood today. Don't you yearn for it? To not have to fight all the time?"

"I do," Aralane answered. "But I must protect."

"Who are you protecting? Madelyn? She stands here, safe and sound."

Madelyn, meanwhile, searched the ship as best she could from this distance. Where was Peter? What had happened to her friend?

Grandma whimpered. With a groan, Madelyn knelt next to her. She kept her cutlass ready. A long black burn mark lay on Grandma's cheek.

"Thank you, Madelyn." She smiled weakly through tears. "It's been a long time since I suffered iron poisoning." She swallowed, fighting back pain. "I forgot how strong the call was."

"What call?"

"The call of the Throne. Why do you think fae rulers are all so cruel? Because their Thrones will do whatever it takes to rule. This close to Fae, just over the Bridge, the Throne called to me. It made me more and more what I once was. Only iron poisoning broke the Throne's hold. Forgive me, Granddaughter." Her tone was so, so gentle now.

Madelyn squeezed Grandma's hand. She didn't understand about the Thrones, but they would work through it. She was just glad to have her grandma back. "What about Peter? Is there something calling him, too?"

"Oh, I think so." Grandma closed her eyes. "But I think what calls him kneels beside me."

"Me?"

"He went wild when he woke, from what I'm told. He would do anything to make sure you were safe."

"Well, I'm safe. He can stop being wild now." Madelyn rolled her eyes and leaned on the rail to stand. She searched the area for Peter.

Something bubbled beneath the crashed sky-ship.

"The plan," Grandma said from where she lay, "was that he would bury himself under the skyship and lift it up, separating the pirates from everyone. The soldiers were just a distraction to get him close enough."

"Lift up the skyship? How? He's from House Grave."

Captain Carangth swore again.

"What?" Madelyn asked, her eyes wide in panic.

"House Grave isn't just decay, Granddaughter. It rules over decaying things. Like mud."

"And we're in a marsh," Madelyn finished.

The skyship lifted into the sky on a column of muck. Water dripped from it. The many still on the ship cried out in surprise. Mud flowed down the sides of the column. At the top of the column, fingers formed, grasping the ship's hull.

"I'm the only one who can stop him, aren't I?" Madelyn asked.

Grandma nodded.

"Aye, I suppose so," Carangth agreed. "Get out there. While you're there, I'll wed Renity and Rapsod. Then it'll be over."

"Someone from your crew's marrying a human?" Grandma asked, finally struggling to sit up.

"Aye." Carangth glanced over his shoulder to where Rapsod stood with his arm around Renity.

Grandma followed his gaze. "Well. That hasn't happened in a long time."

"We don't have time for this. Peter's going to crush the ship and everyone on it. Help me over the rail." Madelyn reached out to Carangth.

He helped her over the edge. Renity's arms were there, too, supporting her. She stood once more on the path to the ship. She took a step and crumpled to the ground.

She'd fought for too long. Her body was giving out. All the injuries from the iron were taking their toll.

No.

Madelyn gritted her teeth. She would not allow herself to fall like this. She could stop Peter. He didn't realize she was safe. He thought he had to protect her. He thought the pirates were enemies. He thought he'd failed. Like Gjemb failed to protect her sisters. Like how Renity couldn't protect her from the iron. She'd been wrong. They both had. And Peter was just as wrong.

Peter hadn't done everything right, but even so, he'd done all he could. He was not a failure. Now Madelyn had to help him see that. He needed to know she was safe.

Madelyn forced herself to her feet. She swayed, but she stood. One step. Another. She could do this. All she had to do was get to Peter. Her boots dragged against the ragged stone path leading out to the tower of muck. They sloshed in the mud.

Her foot slipped. She fell toward the water. She pushed her hands out to catch herself without thinking. They impacted the water's surface. Her wrists screamed in pain. She screamed.

Water flooded her mouth. She tried to inhale air so she could cough but only sucked in more water. She flailed. One hand struck the muddy bottom of the marsh. Her wrist flared with pain again. Which way was the surface? Her eyes were open, but it was so hard to see. Too much mud had been kicked up.

This was so stupid. She was Madelyn of the Sky, and she was going to drown in a marsh that was only a few feet deep. People would laugh at that. The last thing they'd remember about her would be a joke.

215

Something wrapped around her arm and heaved her up. She broke the surface and coughed. She sucked in air and coughed again and again. Murky water streamed from her hair and face. She blinked in the silver light.

Renity held her.

"You're supposed to be getting married," Madelyn choked out.

"Can't get married unless you're there, sis," she said. "And you gotta deal with that twerp first."

"Thank you," Madelyn said.

She rested for a moment in Renity's embrace. "Now, we need to get back to the stone path. Think you can help me down toward Peter's pile of mud?"

"Only if you let me whack him."

"I've never stopped you."

They splashed back to the stone path. Madelyn hadn't gone far from it in her flailing. With some difficulty, they both climbed onto it. Madelyn leaned on Renity.

"You're really heavy, you know that?" Renity said.

"The captain taught me some words I'd really like to use on you right now," Madelyn said.

Renity laughed as they struggled down the path.

And then they stood in front of the pile of mud. The skyship above creaked under the pressure as the mud crushed its sides.

Madelyn took a deep breath. If she couldn't calm Peter down, this would be it. He'd crush the pirates in the boat, along with Prince Aralane and a bunch of innocent soldiers.

She hoped she could do this.

CHAPTER TWENTY-SEVEN

P eter," Madelyn called as she leaned on Renity. The tower of mud didn't respond as far as she could tell. She still didn't know where Peter was.

She called again, "Peter! I'm here!"

This time, something in the mud shifted. A dirty face appeared. Peter's.

"Peter. I'm safe. You don't have to hurt them," Madelyn said.

He blinked at her. "They hurt you," a muddy voice answered.

"I'm safe, Peter. Set the skyship down. Don't hurt anyone." Madelyn tried to keep her voice calm.

"They took you away. I didn't stop them. I should have stopped them." The mud grew thicker. The water around the tower rippled. Above, one of the boards in the hull of the skyship shattered. Splinters rained down on them.

Madelyn didn't move to protect herself. "Peter. I don't blame you. Everyone fought as hard as they could."

"I was supposed to protect you. That's what I'm supposed to do." His face wasn't just dirty. It was made of mud. His voice grew thicker and thicker.

It was like Gjemb. Gjemb hurt because she lost her vine and all who grew on it. And in her hurt, she had become more and more plant-like, like her House. Now Peter was scared and guilty because he'd lost Madelyn. He was losing himself to his House.

And Madelyn knew how to rescue him.

"Renity. Help me get closer."

"You're already pretty close."

"Not close enough."

She limped forward. Renity did her best to help.

"Peter, come here. Just come here." She unwrapped her arm from Renity's shoulders and hobbled forward another step. She took off her hat and handed it back to Renity without moving her eyes from Peter. "I don't blame you. I forgive you. Come here."

"I should have done better! I'm not good enough!"

"Forgiveness isn't about being good enough," Madelyn said. She held her arms as wide as she could. "Come here."

A Peter-sized glob of mud fell out of the tower at Madelyn's feet.

She bent down and wrapped her arms around it. "Peter. I'm here. I'm safe. You're safe. It's okay. I'm not angry at you. You're enough."

She held him. The mud stained her clothes. It soaked into her hands.

But it didn't matter how filthy he was. This was Peter. This was her friend, and this was what he needed. He just needed to be held.

So she would hold him as long as it took.

Madelyn didn't notice when the rain began to fall. She didn't watch as the mud tower began to melt and dissolve, gently setting the ship back into the marsh. She didn't see Gjemb release Prince Aralane from the rail. She didn't listen as Grandma and Aralane conferred or when Captain Carangth joined them.

She held her friend.

The rain washed away much of the mud on Peter's face. It cleansed his hair and his clothing. It soaked through everything Madelyn wore too. It didn't matter.

Peter's eyes were closed, but he held on to her. She held on to him. Sometimes what pain needs is simply someone to be there. Sometimes all guilt needs is an embrace.

"I'm sorry," he whispered.

"I know," she said. "I forgive you."

He pulled away from the embrace. He searched her face. "Are you sure you're fine?"

"It's going to be a while before I'll be able to walk well, but yes, I'm fine." She grinned. "And now the fighting is done. We didn't have to fight at all. The pirates were looking for something I was willing to give anyway. I wish we had all just talked in the first place."

He shook his head. "But they're raiders."

"They're refugees. Just like me. And you, too." Madelyn looked around.

A circle of people stood around them. Grandma. Prince Aralane. Captain Carangth. Renity. Rapsod. They all waited.

"If you're quite through here, I think it's about time for a wedding," the captain said, looking down at them.

Peter jumped. "What? A wedding? But she doesn't even like me, she said! Really? This is really sudden. I'm not sure I'm ready for that!"

The crowd laughed.

Renity reached for Rapsod's hand. Their fingers entwined. "Let's go to the Bridge," she said. "I want to marry the man who chose to dance with me."

CHAPTER TWENTY-EIGHT

G jemb grew flowers from the marsh. Grandma and Madelyn wove them into Renity's
hair. Guri tried to raise gems to use in a ring,
but the iron poisoning kept her from doing anything. Stuhi called a warm breeze to dry everyone
off. Aralane and Peter listened intently as Captain
Carangth gave Rapsod advice for a good marriage.

"And how would you know how to have a good
marriage, sir?" Rapsod asked with a wink.

Carangth shook his head. "Lad, that's a tale for
another sea."

When it was time, the other six skyships descended. They hovered on the Fae side of the
Bridge. Prince Aralane and his men stood at attention on the human side. Grandma and Peter stood
with them.

Renity peered at her wavering reflection in the water below the Bridge. "A bride's supposed to be pretty!" she said. "This is stupid. Rapsod doesn't actually like me, does he?"

Madelyn grinned. "You're the one who's being stupid. He likes you. Even when you look like a drowned rat."

"Hey! It's your fault I was covered in mud."

"You can take it out on Peter later. Now come on. I want to stand next to you so I can smack you when you forget what you're supposed to do."

"Well, I can handle kissing him already."

"Renity!"

"What? A little kissing never hurt anyone. I saw the way you and Peter were looking at each other."

Madelyn whacked her.

Standing between the two groups, Captain Carangth cleared his throat. "I think everyone's tired of waiting," he called.

Renity blushed. She walked toward him. Madelyn followed, holding a bouquet of bright red flowers that Gjemb had grown. They matched the blooms in Renity's hair.

From the other side of the Bridge, Rapsod approached. He grinned. He bowed to Renity. "My lady. I would dance with you."

Renity sputtered. "Now?"

The captain chuckled. "This is how it is at a fae wedding, miss. It's to be a time of joy. So dance."

"I, uh, I've never danced in front of people before."

"Yeah you did!" Madelyn spluttered. "On the ship!"

"I had a sword then!"

"So?" Rapsod held out his hand. "The only one you have to impress is me, and you already do, no matter how you dance today. You followed me. You refused to let me go. No one's ever chased me. So now, shall we dance together?"

"It was a lot easier when I was trying to kill you." Renity laughed.

The captain drew his rapier. "Well, miss, I suppose I can help you with that." He handed it over to her.

She took it. "Really?"

Rapsod drew his. "Try to go easy on me."

Madelyn scooted out of the way, closer to the captain. Renity lunged. Rapsod danced away. She followed. Their blades crossed and struck and laughed. They danced around the Bridge.

The captain sighed. "Renity! You want to dance with this scoundrel, even though he smells and snores?"

"He snores?" she cried out, dodging a blow. She shrugged. "I think I can put up with that. I can always stab him if he snores too loud!"

"Rapsod!" the captain barked. "You sure you want a human woman? You going to dance with her, even though she trips and is going to get old and flabby?"

"Hey!" Renity shouted.

"She might get old and flabby, but I'll dance with her always!" Rapsod worked a bow into his defense and swung in to give her a peck on the lips before dancing away again.

"Hey!" Renity objected again.

"Renity! This man's no good. You deserve someone better!" the captain growled.

Madelyn peered up at him. "This is how fae do weddings?"

"What? Isn't this the way you get married?"

"Well, no. Not that I know of, at least."

"Well, maybe you should think about doing them this way. Renity!" the captain barked. "You deserve someone better!"

"Maybe. But this one'll do."

"Hey!" Rapsod objected.

"Rapsod!" the captain bellowed. "You deserve someone better!"

"Oh, I surely do. But I'm sure I deserve to be punished for something I've done, and this woman might as well do it." He swung in for another peck.

"You get back here!" Renity screamed.

The captain roared laughter. "Renity and Rapsod, you two are stuck together until one of you dies! Go kiss each other, would you?"

Their dance ended. They fell into each other's arms. Madelyn blushed at how deeply they kissed each other.

"Hey! I thought I was supposed to do something!" she said.

"Maybe in a human wedding. Not for us!" The captain slapped her on the back. "These two are wed!"

The Bridge glowed with a bright golden light for a moment and then faded.

"I hope you're happy, Granddaughter," Grandma said as she hobbled closer. Prince Aralane and Peter flanked her. "The pirates are part of our world now, and we're a part of theirs. The Bridge'll see to that."

"We'd already made a deal," Madelyn said. "This just makes it more solid, I guess. We're going to provide a haven to Captain Carangth's crews. They're going to bring us supplies. And Gjemb, if I can convince her, is going to cultivate our land. Make it grow far more food."

"I would, but you'd have to ask me first," Gjemb said as she approached. "Do all humans not grown from the vine breathe each other in like that?" She eyed Renity and Rapsod, still deep in their embrace.

Peter laughed. "Well, some of them, at least. I've been here long enough to know that it's pretty common."

"You do?" Madelyn blushed.

"Well, not from experience. Yet." He winked at her.

Her blush deepened.

After a while, and with some prodding, the Kenevir and the fae began to mingle. They asked each other questions. One of the soldiers had packed a flute. Gjemb grew a violin for one of the fae. Music floated over the marsh, and across the Bridge, new friends began to dance.

Madelyn peered through the crowd. Renity and Rapsod had vanished to be by themselves.

The captain strolled up next to her. "These humans, these soldiers, are they normal for your lands?"

Madelyn nodded, confused. "Why?"

"There's something familiar about them. Almost like they could be distant cousins." He shook his head. "Well. We're going to cross back to familiar lands tonight. Rapsod's coming with us, but we'll be back to visit your Island soon. Peacefully this time."

"Good. Next time just ask for help. Otherwise, I'll have to fight you again. And now I've got an iron cutlass. Being the best swordsman in seven Houses won't protect you next time."

"Aye, lass. Aye. And thank you. You suffered a great deal of pain to bring us home. Thank you. I would not have taken from you what you gave freely."

Madelyn nodded. "Just ask."

"Well, it's good to meet another leader who isn't so selfish." He held out his hand. "Until we meet again, Madelyn of the Sky."

"Captain Carangth." She took his hand and grinned.

The music continued. Someone produced a tambourine. A few voices broke out in song. The celebration grew more joyous.

Peter ambled over to her. "Care to dance?"

"Nope. Not happening."

He looked hurt.

Madelyn laughed. "No. Look at my ankles. My legs! I can hardly stand!"

"So you'd dance otherwise?"

"I didn't say that."

"Of course you didn't." He rolled his eyes. "Back there . . . Thank you."

"I was never angry at you. I was angry at myself. I should have protected the Island better." Madelyn gazed out over the water.

"And I should have protected you."

"Well, maybe we should just get rid of *shoulds*, huh?"

He looked at her. "Yeah. Maybe."

They leaned on the rail, watching the sun set in the distance. The music rolled over them. People joked and laughed in the background.

Today they'd won. They could have torn each other apart, but they found peace.

Madelyn breathed deeply.

"What're you thinking?" Peter asked.

"That I do wish you'd been with me. You would have enjoyed the adventure."

"Yeah. I was stuck with Grandma."

"See? If I was angry with you, that would have been punishment enough already." Madelyn laughed.

Peter joined her.

They spent the evening together, watching over the marsh, enjoying the sound of the music and each other's company.

Epilogue

L ate that evening, the pirates gathered together. The broken skyship they left behind. Six others sailed back into Fae. Renity watched, her arms wrapped around herself. Her expression wavered between joy and tears.

"He'll be back," Madelyn told her.

"Oh, I know. Just not soon enough. Instead, I have to put up with you."

The soldiers from Kenevir broke camp the next morning. Grandma, Renity, Peter, and Madelyn went with them.

Madelyn looked back, feeling the pull of the Bridge. Maybe part of her really did belong here.

The journey home would be a long one, but now so many people would know how to find the Bridge, from both sides. She contented herself with that knowledge. This would not be the last time someone or something crossed the Bridge from Fae.

Surely that meant more adventure awaited her.

FIRE AND FROSTBURN

SNEAK PEEK

CHAPTER ONE

The woman's roots spread across the orchard. They burrowed through the ground and entangled with the trees. Overhead, branches grew thicker. Oranges ripened. Apple trees budded and bloomed. Figs softened.

Madelyn's mouth fell open. She took off her wide-brimmed hat with its long green feather and ran a hand through her wavy brown hair. It probably wouldn't matter how often she watched Gjemb work, she'd still be amazed.

Beside her, Peter chuckled. "This'll be a real surprise for the delegation."

Madelyn nodded, still staring at Gjemb.

The fae's skin had turned to bark, and her hair lengthened until it became willow leaves. Her roots ran over their feet.

Peter wrinkled his nose. "I don't think I'm ever going to like this."

"Think of it like a hug," Madelyn said. "A plant hug for your feet."

"Yeah, whenever House Thorn and House Grave got together, their hugs tended to turn people to dirt." He shivered. "Sorry. I just don't like roots around me. Makes me think I've been asked to serve as a test subject for one of the bosses." He rubbed some of the ever-present dirt from his cheek.

Madelyn looked down at the roots. "Oh. Thanks. Now I'm thinking about that, too."

Trees continued to progress through several months' worth of growth around them. Branches bent under loads of fruit. Gjemb's roots tangled around Madelyn's ankles and climbed up to her knees. The tendrils tickled at her. She tried not to think about what Peter had just said.

She wasn't successful. The brushing sensations turned into spider legs in her mind.

She whacked Peter.

"What? What'd I do?"

"I was happy until you had to open your fat mouth!"

"My mouth isn't fat!" He crossed his arms. "It was your idea to come out here and watch Gjemb."

"You didn't have to come along." Madelyn balled her fists, willing herself to not shiver. She was almost successful. "You usually don't."

"You were nervous. I thought I'd help."

"This is helping?"

"I said I *thought* I'd help." He looked down at the roots as they crawled up to his thighs. "Does she usually, um, tree herself this much?"

"No. I think she's trying to make sure we can impress the ministers from Kenevir." She pressed her lips together and focused on a branch bending under the weight of fresh oranges. "You know, if we can show them fruit they can't grow down there, if we show we can trade with them, maybe it'll help."

The oranges continued to swell.

"Do all fae do that?" she asked.

"What?"

"Turn themselves into other things when they're, um, doing their thing?"

Peter gulped as the roots reached his waist. "Are you sure this is safe? I mean, she's not going to eat us with her roots or anything? Break down our tissues?"

"Not helping."

"So, yeah, if you lose yourself in your House's domain, you can become whatever it is your House presides over. Some people say that's why Fae is called Fae. Because there isn't anything that wasn't once one of us."

"So you'd become dirt?"

"Why do you think I always have dirt on my face? It's just part of who I am." The roots tickled the young fae's elbows. "Seriously. Can we wake her up now?"

"I've never been able to wake her up. She just goes and does her thing."

"Didn't you hug her once?"

"Yeah. That's when she was upset. She isn't upset now. Now she's just really tree-y." Madelyn spotted some new trees sprouting amid the thick grass. A hedge of blackberries had started to rise around them. "Yep. I'm creeped out now."

"Go hug her!"

"Would tearing at these roots hurt her, do you think?"

"Do I look like I'd know?"

"So what's going to happen to you? Are you going to turn into dirt if you keep decaying things?" Madelyn focused on their discussion. She had to distract herself. Gjemb would come back, she reminded herself. She would be fine. What could a few roots and leaves do anyway? Of course she was fine. Was it getting hard to breathe? Madelyn found herself panting for breath.

"Yeah. That's what happens to old fae if they're not careful." Peter's voice cut through Madelyn's swirling thoughts. "The oldest fae become the Thrones for their Houses."

"So I'm going to become a statue?"

"A very pretty statue!"

Madelyn burst out laughing. "Would you stop saying things like that?"

"It's not my fault I can't lie!" Peter craned his neck away from the encroaching roots. "You really would make a pretty statue. Princes would come and swear to free you from the evil enchantment, never realizing you had used your powers to save the world!"

The picture wrapped around Madelyn's mind. An image of using everything in her, turning herself to stone bit by bit. Would she ever do that?

She would. She'd already given so much of herself to protect her Island. Of course she would. There was no chance she wouldn't. She considered the faces of the people she loved. Grandma.

Renity. Essica. Miah. Or the people on the land, like Straeva the wisewoman or Prince Aralane. Yes. She'd give herself to rescue them.

The fibrous roots created tangles in her hair.

Yep. It was definitely getting harder and harder to breathe. The roots weren't pressing in on her. She was just panicking. Maybe just a little.

"I really hope your friend comes back to us soon," Peter said.

"Me, too!"

Madelyn squeezed her eyes shut as the tips of the roots explored her face. They were all over her now. She heard the fruits swelling and the calls of songbirds. A breeze caused the trees to clap their leaves together. A crackle of growing bark snapped at her ears.

The leaves stopped moving.

It felt as if the orchard held its breath. The bark stopped crackling. The roots stopped exploring Madelyn's face.

They began to recede.

Madelyn gasped as they cleared her face. "Oh. Oh, that's so much better."

"I think I'm scarred for life," Peter muttered as his arms shook free of the vegetative mass. "Remind me not to come out here next time Gjemb visits."

The great wave of roots pulled back into Gjemb's form. Her bark became more skin-like. The leaves on her head thinned and turned back to frizzy black hair. She blinked in the dim sunlight that filtered through the branches above. "Oh. I have overgrown. The joy of stretching branches, of bearing fruit overcame me."

The orchard had turned into more of a jungle of fruit trees and bushes with a few overgrown paths leading through. Madelyn stepped over some low-growing blueberry bushes. "It's all right. We weren't—ah. We weren't." She frowned. "I'm trying to say, 'We weren't worried,' but my mouth isn't working. We weren't." She stretched her jaw and tried again. "We weren't—ack."

Peter grinned. "Well. Looks like you're becoming more fae. You can't lie anymore."

"What!" Madelyn blinked, still trying to get her jaw to work. "I'm not lying! We weren't!" She shook her head. "We weren't!"

"We were worried. Well, I was. And she was panting, all panicking and stuff. So I'm guessing she was worried," Peter said to Gjemb.

245

"I wasn't!" Madelyn coughed. "Seriously. I don't like this."

"Why? What use is lying?" Gjemb asked. "False roots feed no one."

"What? It's not that I like lying. It's that. Well . . ." Madelyn blushed. "I don't like having to tell the truth all the time!"

"Telling the truth and not lying aren't always the same thing." Peter winked. "It's okay. I'll teach you all about it. I know you won't mind spending time with me. After all, you like me."

"I don't like—" Madelyn couldn't finish.

"You trying to say that you don't like me?"

Her blush deepened.

Peter jumped up and down and cheered.

Madelyn didn't think her blush could go any redder. She opened and closed her mouth several times as she tried to find words. Finally, she pressed her lips together, glaring first at Peter and then her feet.

Gjemb turned in a slow circle. "This orchard. It is correct."

Grateful for the distraction, Madelyn asked, "What do you mean?"

"Many fruits. The plants will grow where they wish. This is good for everyone." A smile bloomed on her face. "I am pleased to help your Island flourish."

"I'm happy, too."

"I should rejoin Captain Carangth. Perhaps the other members of the crews have completed their tasks here."

Madelyn nodded. "Sounds good. So how do we get out of this forest you grew?"

About the Author

 Jonathon Mast can't float stones or form them into islands, but he enjoys making worlds out of words.

He loves stories about Zorro, the legendary masked hero, and stories with fae magic. Madelyn of the Sky is a bit of both (minus the mask).

He currently lives in Kentucky with his wife, children, and not enough bookshelves.